PACK MAGIC

WHYCHOOSE HALLOWEEN WITCHES
BOOK TWO

AMELIA SHAW

PROLOGUE

BELLA

Halloween night. One year and one month ago.

The day had come, the day I'd dreaded for so long. My twenty-first birthday and the night I'd promised my friends I'd join them in a spell that could destroy us all. Not that they knew it.

I was the reliable one. The witch that read the labels, looked into the warnings, and heeded the wisdom of the generations that came before us. Not Ruby and Tiffany. They were just excited, eager to see results; whereas I felt ill at ease with the whole situation.

I loved them to death—they were the closest things I'd ever had to sisters—but they had to know there was a reason this spell book had been hidden from us. The magic inside was powerful and payment would be demanded if the spell was ultimately successful.

"So, are we going to do this, or not?" Ruby asked, staring at Tiffany and I in turn. "Because there's no going back after this."

Her grin made my stomach drop.

Don't I know it.

Growing up fatherless, the only children of three heartbroken witches, had been hard on all of us. So, years ago, when Ruby had found an ancient spell book belonging to her mother hidden under the stairs, we'd read it. Of course. What kind of teenage daughter wouldn't?

In its pages we'd found an incantation that guaranteed we'd be able to avoid the heartbreak of our mothers before us. Like my best friends, at the time, I'd readily agreed to cast it with them, when we were old enough to want our soul mates to find us. And were powerful enough to pull it off.

After that night, I'd done my due diligence and dived into research, only to realize that terrible things happened to witches who dared to use this particular spell. It was a complicated incantation and required a significant well of power to bring to fruition. Which was why all three of us would need to do it. *Together.* There was no way that any of us could work this spell alone.

My friends believed the benefits far outweighed the risks... but I had my reservations.

The wind moved through the trees around us, rustling the leaves. A fall storm was well and truly on its way and if we were out here too much longer, we'd be caught in the rain. I'd asked my parents if Tiffany, Ruby, and I could use the cabin for our birthday. It was my grandparents' old house, and conveniently in the middle of nowhere.

It was perfect for secret nights like this one. No one would be able to see us here. And as long as we never uttered a word about our activities tonight, nobody would ever know that on our joint twenty-first birthday we'd conducted a spell to call our true loves into our lives.

Tiffany nodded fiercely, agreeing that it was time to start the spell.

I bit my lip as anxiety raced through me. *Shit.* I couldn't be the one to pull out and disappoint my two favorite people in the world.

Ruby rolled her eyes at me. "Come on, Bella. You know we can't do this without you."

She meant that quite literally, unfortunately. Despite my personality falling toward the quieter, more bookwormish type, I was a decidedly powerful witch and without my magic, Tiffany and Ruby couldn't manage a spell of this magnitude.

I frowned and swallowed hard against the worry that tightened my chest. I narrowed my eyes at her, mimicking her expression.

Ruby pouted at me, her gaze becoming plaintive. "Come on, Bella. *Please.*"

I sighed internally. We'd been talking about this spell for years, planning every part of the complex incantation. Waiting until the night we were old enough, powerful enough, and gutsy enough to pull it off.

Despite my better judgement a stubborn resolve settled over me. I couldn't disappoint my two friends. Not now. "Okay, Ruby. I'm in. Let's do this."

Ruby grabbed our hands, and Tiffany followed suit, reaching for my free hand to form a perfect triangle of strength.

We were three witches born on the same day, the most powerful and sacred day of the year for our kind: All Hallows' Eve. We'd literally grown up together, strong, bonded, and loyal to a fault. Our mothers always said we were Fated—blessed—and I believed it.

We clasped hands and glanced down at the ancient book that lay spread open on the ground between us, the spell book Ruby had found years ago, hidden amongst her mother's things.

Fear whistled through me, but I pushed it down and away. This spell would take everything I had, and for these girls—my sisters—I would give it.

As a small coven, a trio of witches, we began to chant in the ancient language of the warlocks and witches that had come before us, a dialect long lost to time and memory.

I concentrated hard on my lines, reading from the book. I hadn't memorized the spell out of fear. I spoke my part and my friends said theirs. Each verse of the spell was a call to the magic that rippled in our veins—to Fate—and most of all, to the unconditional love that we so desperately desired and craved.

Over and over, we chanted our words, our rhythm growing, while the magic in our blood, in our very ancestry, simmered, ready to burst at the seams.

The stress of the spell pummeled down upon us, and I glanced at my best friends.

Tiffany's lips were turned down into a frown.

And Ruby had sweat rolling down her face.

I couldn't stop the spell now, and I wouldn't. In fact, I pushed harder, channeling more of my own power into it. I could feel the words draining my energy at a frightening rate, but pressing my heels into the grass beneath me, I grounded myself and pushed back.

With my strength I knew I could handle more than my fair share of the load. So, I did. I just hoped that Tiffany and Ruby would make it to the end of the spell if I successfully carried most of the pressure. We couldn't stop now, even if we wanted to. There were far too many risks associated with this spell, and not finishing it was just as treacherous. The spell must be completed!

The power of our combined magic swirled around us, alive and violent like a hurricane. I clung to the hope that this spell offered us. It would change our destinies. After this night, we'd never end up like our mothers—abandoned and alone. That in itself had to be worth whatever payment the spell demanded, surely?

The ancient book floated in the space between us, glowing and powerful. I watched it defy gravity with a growing sense of dread.

Ruby opened her eyes, her gaze locked on the book, too.

Tiff grinned.

Relief shot through me. Obviously, what I was doing was working! They were handling the smaller parts of the spell they were carrying.

Buoyed on, we chanted louder, the words in our hearts building naturally as the spell came to a great crescendo. I stared in awe at our joined hands as a bright white light shone between our clenched fingers.

There was a sudden surge of power, and a growing sense of urgency filled the air. We were almost there! We uttered the final words of the spell as a group. The white magic we'd conjured shot into the air above our heads with a cosmic *boom*, exploding in a spectacular eruption of color, like fireworks, sparkling against the dark night sky.

The impact of the explosion blew us back with surprising force. I landed with a heavy thump on the grass, my magic draining away like sand through an hourglass until I could barely open my eyes. I closed my eyes and permitted myself a moment of rest. *The spell had worked.* It must have. I definitely wouldn't have felt so terrible and weak, if it hadn't.

I just needed another minute to collect myself.

"Is that it?" Ruby asked.

Before I could answer, the spell book that had been hovering in the air dropped and landed in the dirt between us with a heavy thump. The front cover closed by itself, all signs of magic, gone.

Tiffany jumped up, groaning as she brushed the dirt from her tight pants.

I took a deep breath, readying myself to stand. I didn't want my friends to know just how much of the spell I'd taken on myself. They'd feel guilty if they knew, and it wasn't their fault that they weren't as naturally strong I was.

Ruby began to rise.

I forced myself to my feet, too. I staggered a little, but recovered quickly and the other two didn't seem to notice. Relief filled me. The moment I'd been dreading all these years was finally over. Now, all we had to do was wait for the spell to come to fruition. For the men —our men—to seek us out.

"So... back to the house for a celebratory drink?" Ruby asked.

I sighed. I seriously needed sleep, but I couldn't be a spoilsport. *It was our twenty-first birthday after all.*

"Sounds like a plan," Tiffany said, flicking her long blonde hair over her shoulder.

Then together we turned and trekked our way back to the cabin.

Once inside, we flicked on the lights and used our magic to mix up cocktails with the colors of the sunset—red, orange, yellow, and a splash of dusky purple.

"Perfect," Ruby said as she picked up her glass that had been resting on the counter.

Tiffany and I plucked up our drinks as well and clinked them with Ruby's.

"Happy birthday," we chorused.

I'd always personally loved sharing a birthday with my two best friends. I never fancied being the center of attention, but Ruby and Tiffany sure did.

We all took a sip of our first legal drink and mutually grimaced at the sheer amount of liquor Ruby had poured into the mix. I gasped, my throat burning.

"Wow, that's strong," Tiff said, blinking rapidly as if to clear her eyes of the burning vapor.

I gulped awkwardly and couched, shuddering before I set the drink back down firmly on the counter. I needed something to eat and soon. My energy was about to burn out completely like a spent candle.

With what little magic I had left, I took a quick breath and waved my hand over the table in front of us, conjuring up a whole feast of savory and sweet snacks to celebrate. Chips, chocolate cake, cookies, and crackers with cheese littered the surface in front of us.

I slumped, exhausted, then slid onto a stool at the kitchen counter. I was done.

"Oh, perfect. Thanks, Belle!" Ruby said, grabbing a handful of chips and stuffing them in her mouth without an ounce of shame.

I sighed and forced myself to pick up some candy and suck on it. I needed the sugar hit in a big way.

"What's up, Bell-Bell?" Ruby asked me.

I glanced at my friend. Her brow was furrowed. She was worried about me.

"Do you think it worked?" I managed to ask, the only thing I could think of to say.

Ruby shrugged. "I don't know. I hope so. I mean, I guess we'll find out."

We certainly would...

"I hope so, too!" Tiffany said, her tone exasperated. "We've only been planning this since forever."

Ruby summoned some extra stools, and then the other two sat down with me, around our tasty birthday spread.

We chatted and ate, drank and laughed, celebrating the fact we had our whole lives ahead of us. I was at college, the only one of the three of us, but still wasn't sure what I wanted to do with my degree just yet.

I leaned forward and rested some of my weight on the counter, happy to let Tiffany and Ruby carry the conversation while I rested a little.

It was kind of strange to think that somewhere out there, our magic was finding its way to our soul mates. I'd never even dated a guy before, so what was I going to do with the one that wanted to marry me? Would I know him on sight? Would he recognize that I was the right woman for him straight away, or would the normal laws of dating apply? Would it just give us the opportunity to figure it all out once we'd met? Or would it be an instant, Fated love kind of thing?

I had a ton of questions, and not a lot of answers or information to go on. But what I did know for sure was, I wasn't dating anyone at all until my soul mate showed up. I would trust in our magic and wait for the spell to manifest. I wouldn't end up like my mother; sad and alone, and still desperately pining after the man who had abandoned her over twenty years ago.

I wouldn't. This love spell was powerful and off limits for a reason. I had to believe that it would see to it—that it would fulfil its promise. All I had to do, just like my friends, was be patient and endure the waiting game. No matter how long it took.

BELLA

A few days before Thanksgiving.

I glanced around Kathy's lounge room, looking from Ruby to Tiffany, then back at our mothers lined up on each side of the room. I could have cut the tension in the room with a knife. Although, seeing as we were all witches, a relaxing spell would probably have been better for the stress.

"Girls, you have to understand that what you did was dangerous," Ruby's mother began to lecture.

I stifled the sigh that rose in my chest. I knew what was coming.

We'd been called to Ruby's house under the pretense of having 'a chat' but really, our moms just wanted to yell at us for the love spell we'd cast last year on Halloween.

Sherie pushed up from the couch where she'd been sitting and moved to the front of the lounge room, standing before the cold fireplace. "Every person who has ever worked that spell has had to endure dire consequences. Just look at what happened to Ruby." She pointed to her daughter as though our friend's happiness—having found not one, but *three* Fated Mates—was a bad thing.

I wanted to refute her claims that we'd done something terrible, but I kept my mouth shut. I wasn't ready to jump into the fray of this lecture yet. I needed more information before commenting.

Tiffany, on the other hand, never thought twice before butting in with her opinion. "You're blaming us for what happened to Ruby?" She said as she jumped to her feet to confront our moms. "Rubys happy! She found her soul mates. But if you really want to blame someone for us casting that spell, how about we blame you three for the fact we had to do it in the first place!"

Damn, we got there quick. I grimaced. This was not going to be pretty.

Sherie dropped down onto the couch next to my mom and their faces drained of color.

My mom glanced over at me. "What does she mean, Bella?"

All five witches turned to me.

A flood of heat coursed up my face and I felt even more uncomfortable—if that was even possible. I shrunk back into the sofa. I didn't want to have this conversation. It was one I'd avoided all my life. I gestured at Tiffany with anxiety. "She can explain." I said quickly.

Tiffany put both hands on her hips and stared down at our moms. "How can you not put two and two together? Seriously? All three of us have grown up without fathers. We've had to grow up seeing you all single and miserable our whole lives and it's been hard! We don't want that for ourselves or our children. We want…" Tiffany stopped, her voice stuttering to a halt as she swallowed hard, a sheen of tears in her eyes as anger gave way to sadness.

Ruby wasn't moving a muscle, and I could see how close to tears she was as well.

Damn. It was my turn to speak. I had to explain and try to salvage this shitty situation we'd found ourselves in. I stood up and reached for Tiffany's hand, threading my fingers in between hers and squeezing tight. "We found the spell book a few years ago," I began. Well, technically, Ruby had, but there was no way I was laying the blame on her. "And it said that the spell would attract our true soul mates to us. None of us wanted to date anyone else except the men we're meant to marry. And after watching the three of you survive the past twenty years heartbroken and alone, we wanted to avoid that, if it was possible."

Mom stared at me; her mouth open. "But, Bella, you know how much power is required for a spell like that. It was dangerous. How did you even pull it off?"

"There's three of us," Ruby said, standing up and joining in the conversation. "We did it together."

My mom's gaze slid to Ruby, then back to me as though Ruby hadn't spoken at all. "Bella? How'd you do it?" she repeated.

I bit my lip. "Um, I just helped as much as I could."

"You mean, you shouldered more than your fair share?" my mother accused, her mouth twisting in a way that showed both concern and a measure of pride.

I shrugged and licked my lips, trying to brush the accusation aside. "We all did the best we could, Mom."

Ruby reached out and grabbed my hand, the one that wasn't already holding Tiffany's. "What did you do, Bella?" she pressed, her brow furrowed.

I shook my head. "Nothing special. The spell just required a lot more power than I'd originally estimated, and I needed to throw in a little more than I expected. That's all."

Ruby stared at me, then the light of comprehension dawned in her eyes. "No wonder I didn't have a hope of undoing the spell without you."

I squeezed her hand, offering her my support in return. "But you did! You managed it without any help at all."

She chuckled awkwardly. "Maybe, but it almost killed me."

I inhaled sharply, pain squeezing my chest at the thought of losing one of my best friends. "Please don't do anything like that ever again. You could have asked me. I would have helped you with anything you needed then, and I still would, now."

"I know, but there wasn't time. Well, I didn't think there was anyway." Ruby turned back to our mothers again. "Does that mean that Bella is going to cop more of these so-called 'consequences' for using the spell?"

I bloody hope not.

The three mothers exchanged glances, worry clear in the lines on their pale faces.

My heart dropped. "Great."

Mom looked to me. "Not necessarily. I'm more interested in the fact that you have more power than Ruby and Tiffany. I mean, I've always known of course, but..."

"Does this have something to do with the fact that my father was a wolf shifter?" Ruby burst out, shocking the whole room into silence.

I gasped and turned to stare at her. "Seriously? When did you find that out?"

How could that be? *None of us could shift.* We were all full witches... weren't we?

"Mom told me, the night of Halloween," Ruby said, then grimaced in apology. "Sorry I haven't caught you up on that. My brain's been a bit scrambled with everything's that happened." She made a whirling signal next to her head with her fingers.

I nodded, a shiver of premonition sliding down my spine. I turned back to our parental units. "Mom…"

She gulped visibly. "Yes, Bella?"

"Was my father a warlock?" I'd been told he was, and it had always made sense that he would have been. Even now. I was more powerful than Ruby, and Tiffany too for that matter. My magic gave me the sense that I wasn't going to like the answer that was about to spill out of my mother's mouth.

Tiffany seemed to understand why I was asking and rounded on her own mother as well. "What about my sperm donor, then?" she asked boldly.

I flinched at her choice of words, but Tiffany had always used humor to deflect from anything serious or hurtful.

Mom, Sherie, and Kathy looked at each other, their eyes wide and wary.

Oh no, this was a secret they all shared, which could only mean…

"Mom," I said, adopting my serious tone of voice. "Please answer the question. Who, or more likely *what* species, were our fathers? You all led us to believe they were warlocks."

Mom waved her hands at us. "Girls, sit down, or we'll stand up. But please don't stand over us. We aren't the ones in trouble here."

I raised my eyebrows. *We'll see about that.* I tugged at Tiffany and Bella. "Come on. Let's sit."

Tiffany's barely leashed anger vibrated through the room in response.

"Let's hear them out." I tugged harder and managed to get both of my friends to sit their butts back down onto the sofa beside me. I knew beyond a shadow of a doubt that the answer to this question was going to change the course of our lives forever. "Okay, we're listening. So, tell us," I said, clenching my teeth in preparation for what was to come.

Sherie stood up and paced to the front of the room again. "I'll go first," she said. "Because Ruby already knows about her parentage. Her father was a wolf shifter and a pure blood from what I understand, which is why I was worried that she might have exhibited signs of being part wolf when she was younger. But as it turns out, she never did, and won't now that she's reached full maturity. But when she brought home a wolf shifter for a soul mate, it made sense to me."

Sherie's lips kinked up at the sides. "I didn't expect three of them of course but considering the curse—I shouldn't have been surprised."

"What curse?" I asked, narrowing my eyes.

Sherie slapped a hand over her mouth suddenly as though she'd revealed more than she was meant to, her eyes wide and panicked.

"Great, even more secrets," I muttered under my breath.

My mom stood up, directing Sherie to take a seat. "We can talk about that later. First things first."

Mom took a deep, steadying breath and stared at me, then Tiffany. "I think the easiest way is to explain is that all three of your fathers... were first cousins."

Ruby jumped to her feet. "They were what?" She whirled on us. "Do you know what that means?" she said, her face pink with excitement and wonder. "We all have wolf shifter dads, which means we could all have soul mates from the pack! Or you guys might even have three like me." Ruby sounded positively elated by the idea and clapped her hands.

My own immediate reaction was quite different. My stomach twisted and lurched, upset by the new revelation. How I saw myself, my genetic makeup, had been turned on its head in a heartbeat. I was part wolf shifter. I wasn't a real, pure-blooded witch. *Damn it.*

Tiffany stood up, grinning like a loon. She obviously didn't mind the idea of mixed blood. "Three wolf shifter mates sounds good to me."

I could only see one silver lining to this dark cloud. "You know what it also means?" I said to them, getting slowly to my feet.

Now our sister-like friendship made more sense than ever before.

No wonder we loved each other so much and felt so connected, even though we weren't related. *Or we hadn't thought we were, anyway.*

"What?" Ruby asked, her expression bright.

"We're related," I said. "If our fathers were all first cousins, then we're officially second cousins, all of us." I'd always thought of these two girls as my soul sisters, my best friends. Now, they were more. *They were literally family.*

Tiffany cried out happily and hugged Ruby and me to her.

I let my cousins, my best friends, hold me tightly, but inside, my heart was aching. I felt betrayed. My mother had lied to me all these years. I had wolf shifter in my blood.

A rough cough made us break our embrace. It was my mom.

"I'm glad you're all happy about your relationship because it's a very special bond, even without the blood link. We always believed that the three of you were meant to be. Your linked birthdays meant that you were supposed to be born together."

"But...?" I led her to continue. I had a feeling there was more to it.

Mom smiled at me. "But your father, Bella, *was* part warlock. He was related to..." she desperately glanced at Sherie for help.

"Darren," Sherie offered.

Ruby's mate! The one with one quarter warlock genes, and three quarters wolf shifter.

"Yes, thank you. Darren, I believe," Mom finished.

Ruby looked at me. "Really? Well, that's kind of cool. Our kids are going to have all sorts of crossed over relationships at this rate."

I swallowed hard. We weren't finished yet. "So, tell me the real story of my father then. Did he actually abandon you like you always said?"

Sherie stood up next to my mom. "All three of us were dating your fathers in secret. We knew the Coven wouldn't understand. The high warlock hated the wolf shifter packs in the area. We weren't allowed to go anywhere near them."

"Then how did you even meet?" I asked. Then I waved my hand.

"No. Forget that part. I don't care." I shook my head, angry. The details didn't matter. What mattered was that everything I'd been told all my life was a damn lie. "So, you were actually dating my father. You weren't abandoned by some random stranger?" I lashed out. Which in retrospect was a much better tale and made more sense as to why my mother had never dated anyone else.

My mother shook her head slowly. "No. I was totally in love with him. He was half wolf shifter and half warlock. His mother was a witch the pack had taken in, so I don't know why our high warlock hated wolf shifters so much when they seemed to be accepting of us at the time."

I filed that piece of information away for another day. Maybe the witch who'd married the shifter all those years ago had been related to the high warlock? Or was meant to marry him and chose a shifter instead? Who knew at this point? They were all gone, or dead. I wouldn't be able to ask them.

"So, what happened? Why did they disappear?" That seemed to be the most pertinent part of the story for me. I wanted to know what had happened to our fathers. All three of them.

Tiffany grabbed my hand. "Hang on. Can we back it up? Can I just ask if my dad's a half warlock too?"

I smiled and nodded, but I already knew the answer. There was a reason I was more powerful than Tiffany and Ruby. It was because of my father's mixed blood—he had the most warlock in him.

Tiffany's mom turned to her. "Your dad was a full wolf shifter, honey. Similar to… Billy, I believe. He was Ruby's father's Beta."

The spell and the people involved were all turning full circle. Our three fathers were just like Ruby's triad: two full wolf shifters and a half breed. Now Tiffany and I had to wait to see what men were sent our way. Would we get three as well? Or just one?

My stomach clenched. I wasn't sure I could handle three. That seemed… unmanageable. I still wasn't sure how Ruby did it.

"And you two dated as well?" Tiffany asked.

Tiffany's mom nodded, though her cheeks flared red.

"Mom!" Tiffany said. "Don't lie to me."

"I'm not lying!" Kathy retorted earnestly. "It's just that we'd only just started dating when he disappeared. And I conceived you the very first time we slept together, so I always felt like you were meant to be, Tiffany. Always."

Tiffany slumped toward the couch.

I sighed. There was just too much information coming at us. Too many emotions. And yet I couldn't stop now. I needed to know everything—at least all the major stuff. I focused on my mother once more. "Mom, tell me what happened when our fathers disappeared. *Please*. Has it got something to do with the curse Sherie mentioned before?"

Our three moms joined together again presenting a united front, as though afraid of what was coming next.

I stood firm. I needed to know this. What had happened to my father? Why had my mother spent twenty years alone? Why had I never met him? Or heard his voice? Was even he alive?

When they didn't answer, I persisted. "You all told us that they abandoned you. So, all our lives we've assumed that you had one-night stands with some random assholes who didn't care about you. And those supposed realities drove us to perform the soul mate spell." I glared at each mother, letting the truth of that sink in. "But it seems that was all a lie. You loved them and they loved you. So, our misery was all for nothing. We deserve the truth. So, tell us what happened. Are they still alive? Did they die?"

Ruby gasped, grabbing hold of Tiffany and me as though we were her lifelines or anchor points. "Oh my God, I know who they are! Or were... or whatever."

"Tell me," I said instantly, since my mom didn't seem to want to be honest or more forthcoming.

Ruby's eyes were alight with excitement. "They're the cousins who went missing twenty-two years ago! Jackson and Billy told me about them. Ever since that night, not a single female has been born to the pack. They have all these strong males and no-one to mate with!"

I twisted around to stare at our three mothers, who all looked guilty as hell. I met my mother's gaze defiantly and crossed my arms over my chest. "Sounds like a bloody curse to me."

 BELLA

I tapped my foot impatiently and waited for my mother to tell me I was wrong. But I wasn't wrong. I had a feeling for these sorts of things, and although I was never arrogant about my magic—after all, it was a gift, not something to take for granted—I could feel the premonition and the rightness of my claim.

"Who cursed them?" I asked. "The high warlock?" That sort of spell, especially one big enough to spread through an entire town of people, could only be performed by someone much more powerful than your everyday witch. Then another thought occurred to me. "Or was it the elders? The whole Coven? Tell me."

If my father, Ruby's father, and Tiffany's father had been taken from us because of some misguided curse, I wanted to damn well know about it. I, scratch that, *we* had the right to know!

Ruby slid her hand over my arm. "Calm down, Bella."

I shook her off. "Don't you realize what this means? Our fathers could still be alive!" I twisted back around to stare at our mothers. "Where are they?"

My mom pulled the other moms to their feet, so all six of us were now standing in the small lounge room. It was squashy, and hot, and tempers were flaring.

But we needed to know this.

I needed to know.

"We don't know. When we found out we were pregnant, all of us, we were terrified. We knew the coven would hate it, so we..." Kathy trailed off.

"You went to the high warlock, didn't you?" I accused, knowing exactly where this conversation was going. "Oh, no."

The high warlock, when he came into his role, was given the power of the Coven, the land, and the centuries of magic that was naturally instilled in our people. He could have done anything to us —or our fathers. Literally *anything*.

My mom grabbed my hand, her brows furrowed. "We didn't know what was going to happen, so we went to him seeking help. He'd always been like a father to us, old and wise."

I swallowed hard, strangely aware that I was the leading this conversation. Ruby and Tiffany had faded into the background, observing and listening in relative silence. This was certainly not a role I was used to, or remotely comfortable with, but I pushed on, determined to get to the bottom of this—to the truth, no matter how painful it might prove to be. "And what did he do?" I asked calmly, though I wasn't feeling it at all.

"He offered to help," Mom said, biting her lip the way I did when I was nervous. "He said we could perform a spell to suppress your wolf shifter genes so that you would be accepted by our Coven as full witches."

I could imagine our mothers believing that—they'd been young and scared after all—but obviously something else had gone on.

I clenched my teeth together. "Then what happened?"

My mom's hands shook as she ran her fingers through the tangle of her long hair. "The high warlock conducted his spell, calling on our magic to help him finalize the incantation. We didn't think much of it, to be honest. We just wanted our babies to be healthy. But when we went looking for our secret lovers to tell them about you three, our little miracles... they were gone."

"Gone?" Ruby repeated. "Gone, where exactly?"

Sherie shrugged. "We don't know. We spent months looking for them, and waited, hoping they'd come back—but they never did. And the high warlock never really explained to us what his spell specifically did beyond suppression, or if it did something more than he'd claimed."

Kathy jumped into the discussion. "When none of you shifted during your teenage years, we assumed the spell had done just what he promised, but the timing of the men disappearing... It's always worried us."

"So, then, did you ask him if he did something else?" Ruby asked.

"Of course, we did. Many times, hon," Sherie said. "The high warlock only reiterated that the spell simply stopped our babies from shifting; and if our men had disappeared on us, then that was merely a reflection on their character. But it was..."

"Too coincidental?" I asked, frustrated.

"Especially for all three to go missing at the same time," Ruby added. "What are the odds of that actually happening?"

I shook my head. *Too small to calculate.* Especially considering they were all wolf shifters, paranormal beings renowned for their pack behaviors and lifestyle. Family was integral to their very genetics, to their hierarchical structure. I felt sick. My father had been taken from me. A man who could have loved me and helped guide me through life. He could have continued to love my mother. Our lives would have been so entirely different if he'd been around.

"Do you think they might still be alive?" Tiffany asked quietly, the usual humor and heat behind her words, gone. If anything, she sounded sad. And genuinely more so than I'd ever heard of her being before.

I glanced over at our moms, not wanting to weigh in myself.

Sherie began to speak, *umming* and *ahhing* in a way that told me she had no actual idea of how to respond, probably because she didn't know the truth.

"Hang on a second!" Ruby said, her green eyes glittering. "Did you say my father was an Alpha wolf, Mom?"

Sherie nodded, her lips pursed. "I think so. Like Jackson. Why?"

"Because I saw one, once. When I was little. In the woods near the church. He was big, and gray, and I knew he was an Alpha from the way he moved and his smell. Don't ask me how—I just *knew*. Then, when I met Jackson, I picked up on the same scent coming from him, because he smelled the same. Just like an Alpha."

The whole room fell quiet, not one of us daring to breathe in case the spell around her words popped like an ephemeral bubble.

"You..." Sherie was peering at Ruby as though she'd never laid eyes on her daughter before. She swallowed hard, then tried again. "You saw a wolf in the woods and never told me?"

I shivered, feeling the magic of the truth weaving through the room. We'd always suspected our moms used a spell to make us tell them the truth. And now it was just a habit for us to always tell them. They didn't need to command it anymore.

Ruby shrugged. "I wasn't scared or anything at the time. He seemed strong and nice, in a way. And I knew there were wolf shifters just outside town, so I guessed that he was one of them, and went on my way. I was only like, six or seven. I didn't think it was important."

We were all staring at Ruby now, our gazes locked on her like she was a tasty hot chip, and we were starving seagulls.

Why wasn't she freaking out? Didn't she realize that she probably met her father? The good news was he was probably still alive, or at least had been fifteen years ago. And if he was still alive, then maybe there was a chance that my dad, and Tiffany's dad, were too!

"What?" Ruby demanded, looking around our group as though we were the ones that had gone insane, and not her.

"I've got to sit down," Sherie said, staggering backwards before half falling onto the couch behind her.

"We always thought it was possible, Sherie. You know that," Mom said.

"You always thought what was possible?" I asked my mom. "That they were alive? Or…"

She shook her head. "No, that they had shifted into their wolf forms and weren't able to shift back again."

"What do you mean?" Ruby asked, folding her arms.

"Well, that explained how they were suddenly gone, and how no-one could find them," Kathy said.

"Although, if that was the case, why wouldn't they go back to the pack, or us?" Sherie went on. "Why would they leave?"

"Hang on a second," Ruby said, holding up her hands suddenly, obviously having finally clued into what we were all thinking. "Could that gray wolf I saw when I was little… could that really have been… my father? I just thought since I was related to an Alpha, and that I could recognize their genetics… It never occurred to me that it could have actually been my…" Her eyes shimmered with unshed tears.

It made my throat clog up to see my friend struggle to speak and find the words to say that she may have met her father and not even known it.

"But they didn't know about us, did they?" I repeated to our moms, checking that I had my facts right. Then I turned to Tiffany and Ruby. "Sit. Sit."

They did, exchanging glances with each other.

With everyone sitting again, my brain whirled with information.

I popped up and began to pace around the small living room. "Let me get this straight. Our fathers were related. First cousins. And they were all varying degrees of wolf shifters?" I glanced at our moms, who nodded in response. I turned and headed back the other way, trudging along the worn carpet in thought. "They didn't know you were all pregnant, but disappeared after the high warlock did some sort of spell on you guys?"

Mom nodded. "Pretty much."

I looked toward my best friend, Ruby. "And you said the cousins were never heard from again?"

Ruby chewed on her bottom lip. "I think so. I only heard Jackson and Billy discuss it once or twice. They thought the missing cousins might have something to do with the lack of females born into the pack."

Shit. I'd forgotten about that part. I twisted around to face our moms again. "So, our fathers disappeared, and the pack they're from have no women to breed with? You don't think that sounds like a legitimate curse?" I eyed our mothers one after another. They had to *know* that this sounded suspicious beyond feasibility.

Mom nodded. "Yeah. It does when you put it like that, but we always just kind of..."

The three moms glanced at each other; guilt etched into their faces.

I sighed and pulled the elastic from my ponytail, letting my hair fall around my shoulders. "You chose to ignore it. You had babies to raise, and your men up and disappeared. I guess I kind of get that." I didn't want to judge our moms too harshly, but they could have done something more to find our fathers. *Surely?* I collapsed on the couch between Ruby and Tiffany. "I just can't believe it."

Ruby chuckled. "Which part, Tiff?"

"Well... all of it, really."

Tiffany grinned at me. "I like the part about us possibly having three wolf mates each, though. That'd be pretty cool."

I swallowed hard. *Three men?* "Speak for yourself," I said.

Tiffany laughed. "Don't worry! I am."

"I know." I rubbed my eyes, a headache pulsing along my temples. "I don't know what to do with all this information. It's just too much."

Mom slid to the edge of the couch. "This was supposed to be a conversation about responsibility and magic, but you three managed to hijack it."

I glanced at her, annoyed beyond words. *Irresponsible? Us? Compared to them?* "Mom. You can't be..."

Mom waved her hands at me. "I know, I *know*. You don't have to say anymore. Maybe we should go and give Ruby and Sherie a little privacy? It's been a long night for them."

She glanced at Tiffany's mom who nodded. "Yeah, good idea."

I stood up and hugged my friends—my cousins—my chest aching and tight with unresolved emotion and tension. "I'll message you guys later."

Ruby pulled back and grinned at both of us. "Sounds like you two might need to spend some time at my new house. Your mates could be casually hanging around at the pack... just waiting for you to show up!"

I tried not to flinch. "I'd love to see your new house," I said. But I'd deliberately stayed away from visiting Ruby at Jackson's house, fearing the pack politics and, well, the wolf shifters, themselves.

Tiffany sighed, looking dejected. "I've been out to Ruby's loads of times, and I've never met my guys."

I shrugged. "There's no way of knowing if our soul mates are part of the same pack," I reasoned. "They could be human, or even a wolf shifter from another pack entirely. Surely there's more than just Jackson's pack in the state?"

Ruby nodded. "Yeah, there's at least three within driving distance that I know of."

"See," I said to Tiffany, my stomach clenching at how real this was suddenly all getting. "Don't stress so much. Fate will send your guys to you when they're good and ready."

We said our good-byes and parted ways.

I wandered out the front door with my head hurting.

Mom walked beside me, silent.

Our house was only down the block, but I appreciated the quiet as we walked. *So much had changed.* I looked at my mom. "You know, if we'd known the truth about our fathers and your relationship with them, we would never have cast that spell in the first place."

Mom sighed as we walked up our path and opened the front door. "I know, Bella. And that's something I'm going to always regret." She went inside.

I turned back to look out toward the horizon. To the pack's town within the forest in the distance. Inhaling deeply, I shivered with premonition. Something was moving. *Something was changing.* And whether I was ready for it, it was coming.

CHAPTER 3
BELLA

Come by after you finish classes for the day.

Ruby's message came through on my cell phone as I walked to the car.

Just finished, I typed back. *You okay for me to come now? I can be there in 20 mins.*

Yay! I'll put on some lunch. See you soon.

I laughed to myself as I climbed into my little red beetle and turned the ignition on with a touch of anxiety. I was tempted to ask her what sort of lunch she had planned for us. Was Ruby going to just make some sandwiches? Or would I get there to see her wave her hands around and magic up a feast? I honestly didn't mind either way, though it would be interesting to see what the wolf shifters permitted in their home and town. Would she be able to do magic within the pack's territory?

I drove away from classes and toward my house, but instead of following the highway into town, I made a quick left toward the pack's land. My stomach dropped as I indicated, and I became sicker and more trembly, the closer I drove. Now that I knew this was where my biological father was from my nerves were on high alert. Did I have more cousins in the pack? Grandparents, maybe? *Did I even want to find out?*

When I reached the small set of shops that comprised the wolves' town, I glanced around. There were people about, but it certainly wasn't what I would call busy. Busy or not, Ruby was right about one thing, that's for sure—there were a lot of men. Walking across the road, hanging out at the restaurant, and filling up their vehicles at the local gas station.

Where were all the women? *Oh, that's right. The high warlock cursed them because of us.* All the females would be twenty-three, or older. I wouldn't spot any little girls with pigtails around here.

I followed my phone's map directions, making a few quick turns, before coming to park outside of a large, two-story house. "Whoa. Nice," I said to myself as I grabbed my backpack and climbed out of my car.

This was Jackson's house? This new, family-sized home on a nice street? I nodded approvingly as I clutched my cell and walked up to the front door. I checked the message from Ruby again to confirm the address. The last thing I needed was to come face to face with a wolf shifter I didn't know. I wasn't sure my nerves could take that.

With my heart in my throat, I knocked on the door and a moment later, it flew open to reveal my red-haired friend. Relief swept through me like a tidal wave. *Thank goodness.*

"You came!" Ruby cried excitedly, pulling me into a hug.

"Of course."

She glared at me as she stood back with a dark note of humor. "What do you mean, *of course*? I've asked you to come visit at least ten times over the last month and you've never been able to make it." She pulled me inside and shut the front door behind us.

I glanced around the large living room and new kitchen. "Yeah, well, I was a little intimidated by it all," I said. I still was.

There was a classic spread of crusty, fresh bread rolls, a colorful salad, and some delicious smelling cold chicken on the counter.

I smiled at my friend. "Did you make all this?"

She waved a hand at our lunch dismissively. "Well, I bought the bread rolls from the bakery this morning, chopped up some veggies, and the chicken is from last night's dinner. Though you're lucky I cooked four chickens or there wouldn't be any left for lunch today! Those guys eat so damn much, you have no idea." Ruby shook her head with a secretive, self-indulgent laugh.

I slid onto one of the kitchen barstools with a coy smile. "Want me to make us a drink? Or maybe some dessert?" I lifted my hand.

Ruby reached out to stop me. "No, thank you. It's okay," she said. "I'm trying not to do too much magic around here."

My heart sank. "Yeah, I assumed the wolves wouldn't like it."

Ruby laughed. "Oh no. It's not like that, I promise. The guys are fine with my magic. It's just that ever since Halloween, I've been struggling with my health a little, and Darren's been watching me like a hawk. If he found out I used my magic for anything other than a lifesaving operation? He'd flip out."

I slumped on the stool. "I can use mine though, right?"

"Oh, yeah. Sure. You're good. Go for it." Ruby grinned, excusing herself.

But all the fun had gone out of it now, the moment deflated like a dead balloon. "Nah, it's okay. This is great."

"What's wrong, Bell Bell?" Ruby asked, picking up plates as she began to put together salad and chicken rolls for us both. "You want all the stuff?" She gestured to the lettuce, tomato, shredded carrot, and sliced cheese.

I nodded. "Yes, please. I'm starving."

"So," Ruby said, stuffing our rolls full of all the trimmings. "Talk to me. I've known you long enough to know when something's up."

I sighed and pulled out my hair tie, then ran my fingers through my tangled locks. "I don't know, it's just that… I don't know." How I was feeling at the moment was too hard to put into words.

"You're worried about everything we found out yesterday?" Ruby asked, handing me a plate. "Let's go sit on the couch and you can magic me up some Pepsi Max. The supermarket here doesn't sell it."

I laughed at the simple request and flicked my hand, conjuring up two tall glasses and the bubbly drink. I settled onto the couch and took a bite out of my roll, the soft white bread and crunchy salad making me salivate. "Yum. Thanks. I needed this." I glanced around the white, rather sterile-looking room, then stared at my friend. "It's a really beautiful house, Ruby."

My friend grinned. "I know exactly what you're thinking. It needs some color, right? My mom hasn't visited yet. I'm holding her back. I'm honestly terrified about what she'll do when she sets foot in the place. She's chomping at the bit to come over, but I don't think the boys would appreciate her eccentric sense of style."

I laughed out loud. "Oh my God, she'll have this place whipped into perfectly witchy shape in three seconds flat."

Ruby groaned. "I know. She's coming here for Thanksgiving tomorrow and I've banned her from doing any spells outside of food, because I know what she's like. She'll totally re-paint the whole damn house if I so much as look the wrong way."

I nodded. "She totally would."

Ruby sighed as she looked around. "I like it like this to be honest. White, and clean, and new. Don't get me wrong, it needs a splash of color, some throw blankets and cushions, and maybe even a few choice photos or paintings for the walls; but it's nice to live somewhere so completely different to the house I grew up in."

I blinked down at the sofa and realized it was just as plain as the rest of the house. It had no personality of its own. "Do you mind?"

She shook her head. "Not at all."

"What colors were you thinking?" I asked, conjuring my magic to the tips of my fingers, ready to create.

"Nothing too out there. Maybe purple, black, and silver?"

I cracked my knuckles and wove a spell, creating a throw rug for the back of the sofa, and three cushions, matching the colors Ruby had requested. Then I wiggled my fingers in Ruby's direction and made more cushions for her chair, as well as the one next to her.

"Awesome!" Ruby said, clapping her hands and sighing. "That's great. I love it, thank you."

I glanced at the plain white wall behind her and had an idea. "What color wolves are your guys?"

Ruby tilted her head curiously. "They're black. Why?"

I spoke a soft spell and behind Ruby a framed canvas formed. My beautiful, red-haired friend stood at its center, flanked by three majestic black wolves.

"What do you think?" I asked.

Ruby twisted around and gasped. "Oh, my God, Bell, that's beautiful." When she turned back around to face me, her eyes were shining with unshed tears. "Thank you so much."

I smiled in embarrassment and went back to eating my lunch. When I was finally finished, I picked up my drink to wash it down. "So, you're happy then, Ruby? You look it." I'd never seen my friend so vibrant. So bouncy. Even after the spell that had almost ended her life.

Ruby nodded, pushing a stray piece of shredded carrot into her mouth. "Oh, yeah, the guys are amazing. They're everything I ever wanted. Passionate and funny, loving and affectionate, but tough too."

"Yeah, I can imagine they would be pretty strong." Wolf shifters were part animal after all. Surely that translated into them being rough and even feral at times.

"Not in a bad way, Bell," Ruby assured me. "All I mean is that they seem tough, you know? They're muscly, big, and gruff, but underneath it all, they're total sweethearts."

I lifted an eyebrow at her. "Always?"

Her face turned the color of her hair. "Well, ah, the bedroom stuff can get pretty intense, but in the best way. I want them to be dominant there. I certainly didn't have any idea what to do at the start."

It was my turn to flush red. "I didn't mean like that..."

Ruby laughed at me. "Well, what else did you mean? Surely, you're a tiny bit curious about it all?"

I shook my head. No. I really wasn't. "What you do in the privacy of your own bedroom is your business, not mine."

Ruby opened her mouth to say something, but the front door burst open and the sounds of rumbling, loud men exploded into the previously quiet room.

I jumped at the noise. "What's that?"

"Ruby! We're home. Have you eaten yet? Or... Hello."

I turned around. Three beautiful men stood in the lounge room. I recognized them from the one time I'd met them at Halloween in town, but my heart still hammered in my chest at seeing them again.

"Hello," I managed to say and waved awkwardly.

"This is Bella. I think you guys met once on Halloween," Ruby said. "I invited her around for lunch since she hasn't seen the house, or where I'm living, until now." Ruby got up off her chair with a bounce in her step and went to greet her triad of men.

I watched, unable to look away.

The biggest guy, Jackson, scooped her up and pressed a hard kiss to her lips.

Then they passed her between them, each of the three men kissing and hugging her, not a sign of jealousy or worry.

Seeing them did weird things to my insides, so I looked away, not sure if I was turned on, or stupefied by the turn of events.

"You're Bella. Hey, I'm Darren." The smallest of the three men approached me and held out his hand.

I got to my feet, not wanting to be so far below his eye level.

"Yeah, I am," I said, noticing the swirl of purple in his eyes. "You're the part warlock one."

He chuckled. "Yeah. My grandmother was a witch."

I looked over at Ruby. "So, he's technically related to... me. Wow." I glanced back at Darren, to his stubborn chin and elegant nose.

Darren's eyebrows rose. "I'm sorry, what?"

Ruby tugged Billy onto the lounge with her since he didn't seem to want to let her go. "That's right. I didn't get to tell you guys everything I learnt yesterday. Bella's mom said that the reason Bella is more powerful than me and Tiffany in magic, is because her dad was a wolf who was half witch-half wolf. I think it was your mom's brother, or something like that." Ruby grinned at Darren.

Darren turned to stare at me, his gaze roaming over me in a strangely assessing way, then he grinned, his white teeth flashing. "Nice to meet you, then, cousin."

I chuckled, feeling abashed and put on the spot. "Um, yeah, likewise."

"The Council's going to flip when they find out there's more Manterri daughters," Jackson said, walking over to the food in the kitchen. "Ruby, can we make up some rolls to take back to work with us?"

"Yeah, of course," she called. "Though there's not a lot of chicken left, now."

"Oh, I can fix that," I said and flicked my wrist in the direction of the chicken platter without a thought.

Jackson's sharp gaze snapped to mine. Then his face lit up. "Thanks!" he said appreciatively.

"That's a damn handy trick to have up your sleeve," Billy quipped, joining Jackson in making himself some lunch.

Independent guys. I liked them already.

Ruby glared at them and crossed her arms with a dramatic sigh. "You know, I could magic you up some food too—if you'd let me."

"Don't you dare," Darren said, reaching for Ruby and drawing her into his arms for another kiss. "You can't afford the energy at the moment. Wait until you've fully recovered, then you can do all the magic you want, baby."

A wave of sadness hit me again. "I still can't believe you almost died, Ruby. I'm so sorry I didn't tell you how much strength that spell truly needed. But I couldn't have known you were going to attempt it on your own..."

"What do you mean?" Darren asked quizzically.

I sighed. "Basically, when we performed the soul mate spell, I took on more than my third of the burden to ensure the spell was successful. It was too big for the two of them, Tiffany and Ruby, but it was just as dangerous to stop and let the spell fail as well. So, I..."

"Bella basically took on the full force of the magic. Because she's more powerful, and braver than us," Ruby finished for me with a grin. "But that meant when I went to undo it, I wasn't just tripling the need for my own share of magic. It was in fact way more."

"And yet you still managed it!" I said, a smile flitting to my lips.

She shrugged. "Ultimately, I don't care if my magic's really gone for good at the end of all this. I've got my soul mates. I don't need anything else."

I watched my friend as her men descended on her for more hugs and kisses, this time to say goodbye.

I frowned as Ruby's words registered in my mind. *Was she serious? Was her magic acting up? Did she really think she'd never fully recover? And was that the payment the spell would ask of all of us?* Because I wasn't sure that my magic was something I would be willing to part with.

CHAPTER 4
JONAH

I made my way over to my cousin Jackson's house, looking for my older brother Billy. I'd been told they'd headed home for lunch from the work site, but I needed his help sooner rather than later. So, instead of being afraid like half the pack was of his witch mate, I jogged over to his new house and boldly knocked on the door. Ruby was cool. They all needed to get the hell over their prejudices and meet her—just give her a chance.

"Coming," came a female voice from inside.

I smiled to hear her sounding so happy. The lack of females in the pack was really starting to affect the whole mentality of the town. It was getting tougher, rougher, and harder to live like this. We needed more women. And children. Like... *now.*

The front door opened and my greeting froze on my lips as a wave of pure perfection overwhelmed my senses. I inhaled deeply and closed my eyes on a moan. *Who, or what, was that?* I wondered.

"Make sure you come over tomorrow. Bring your mom too," Ruby was saying to someone inside the house as she pulled the door open wide. Then Jackson's mate turned toward me with a smile. "Hey Jonah. Which of the boys are you looking for?"

If it had been any other day, I would have smiled at Ruby's easy way of talking about her pack of men. But today, all my wolf senses were on high alert, and I struggled to talk. "Billy," I managed, though my teeth had begun to shift, and my inner wolf was howling like mad in my head. And then, looking past Ruby, I got my first look at the woman responsible for my wolf to going bonkers on me.

She stared directly at me.

My heart squeezed tight in a way I've never felt before and I swallowed hard. She had long brown hair, spectacular dark eyes, and beautiful lips.

"Jonah, this is my best friend, Bella. Bell, this is one of Billy's brothers," Ruby said, her happy tone bouncing between us as we were introduced.

"Hello," the beautiful stranger said to me cautiously. "It's nice to meet you."

I tried to talk, but the only thing that came out was a garbled load of crap. Then a growly bark. "Fuck," I spat out, shaking myself.

Bella backed away from me, and closer to Ruby, clearly taken aback.

I didn't blame her one bit. I was acting freaking insane, and there was only one possible reason for it. One entirely all too simple explanation. She was my mate. *Fuck...* There was no other sane excuse as to why I just wanted to grab her, kiss her, shift into my wolf, and run howling through the forest—all at the same time.

"You okay, Jonah?" Ruby asked, stepping in front of Bella like a physical shield and frowning at me.

I stumbled backwards, putting distance between us. My wolf calmed down once I wasn't quite so close to her. I could breathe again, if I couldn't smell her. *God, she smells amazing.* "Um, my shifter is kind of having a hard time around Bella."

Ruby's mouth dropped open and her eyes went wide. "No way!" she gasped. "Does that mean she's your...?"

I looked straight at Bella, noticing the unmistakable purple swirl of her magic and my stomach dropped. Another witch. Of course, she was. *Damn, the elders are going to hate this.* I straightened my spine. *Fuck the elders.* I wanted my mate. Someone to love. Someone Fate chose for me. I didn't care if she had magic or not.

I coughed to clear my throat. "Bella, I need to shift and run. I'm sorry I can't stay and chat. But I don't want to freak you out, so I have to go. Now. Can we have breakfast tomorrow at Milly's? Will you come back?" My gaze slid to Ruby's. "Will you tell her where?"

Ruby nodded excitedly. "Yeah, of course. You don't want to make it dinner tonight, maybe?"

I hesitated. "I want to, but I don't know how my wolf is going to handle this or how long I'll need to shift for. Maybe I should ask Billy—"

"I need to get back home," Bella interjected, her beautiful eyes finding her feet. "My mom's already expecting me for dinner."

Ruby beamed. "Well, that's that then. Breakfast it is. Go on, Jonah. Run!"

I thought I'd at least make it to the end of the street before my wolf ripped through me.

But Bella stepped over the threshold and called out, "Wait! I don't understand."

The wind picked up her scent and sent it spiraling toward me. I inhaled her sweetness like a drug, my eyes rolling back in my head as I practically gagged trying to drag the scent in faster and my wolf whipped up inside me like a hurricane.

One moment, I had full control of him, and the next I was shifting. I staggered further away but couldn't get far enough before my wolf burst forth. I dropped to all fours. My skin sprouted fur, my face morphed and elongated, and my limbs grew shorter. When I was fully transformed and my eyes had shifted to black and white vision, I turned my head and glanced back toward the front door.

Bella stood next to Ruby, clinging to one of the porch balustrades. Her mouth had dropped open in awe and she was staring at me like she'd never seen a wolf shift before. Which she probably hadn't. *Poor girl.* I whined a little, unhappy to be leaving her so soon, but seeing as her nails digging into the wooden porch like she was holding on for dear life, I needed to get going.

I took off, running down the street and away from my mate—away from my future. Billy had said that his mate Ruby had three wolf mates, not just one. And he should know, he was one of them. *Would Bella be the same?* Would I be hanging around just waiting for her number second and third mates to show up? I shuddered as I hit the forest edge and picked up my pace. I didn't want to share my mate like Billy did.

Then again, as a Beta wolf, surely I could cope with an Alpha in our family as well? We only had a few of those in the pack, though I wasn't sure who I wanted to share my home and hearth with. *Hopefully none of them*, was my last thought for a long time as I raced through the forest, hope swelling in my heart. I'd beaten the curse! Despite there being no mate born for me in our pack, Fate had found a way to bring her to me.

～

Bella

I turned around to Ruby, my mouth hanging open. "Did you just see that?" Or had I imagined a gorgeous young man turning up to see Ruby, before turning into a white wolf and running away?

Ruby covered her mouth with her hand and nodded. "Yep."

"He was white!" I said. The most magnificent white wolf I'd ever seen. Not that I'd seen any in my time, not in real life, anyway. "I can't believe it."

Ruby reached out a hand to me, slowly, as though I might spook. "Are you okay, Bell?"

"I..." I placed a hand on my chest, my heart pounding beneath my palm. But I didn't think it was from fear. I felt strangely excited. "I think so..." I said, my gaze still focused off in the distance.

"What is it?" asked Ruby.

I swallowed hard, trying to sort out my jarred thoughts. "I'd assumed that seeing them in wolf form would be crazy scary. But it's not. It's..."

"Exhilarating, isn't it?" Ruby finished for me.

I nodded and swallowed hard again. Adrenaline zinged through my body like lightning or bursts of energy, making me want to run. Which for someone who didn't exercise a hell of a lot, was a truly strange sensation.

"It's weird," I said. "Though I didn't realize they changed like that. I don't know what I imagined. But..."

Ruby chuckled in good humor. "The first time I saw Jackson and Billy in wolf form I almost died. So, you're taking it much better than me."

I really couldn't believe it. I felt alive for the first time in, well, forever. I don't know what had lit up inside me, sparking in a way that changed everything—but I didn't want it to stop. "Well, it's exciting, really," I said. "And now that I know we're related to these... shifters, it makes sense as to why we would feel more connected to them."

I'd honestly been terrified to come here. To meet a shifter in the flesh. Now, I wanted to race after Jonah to see him again. Maybe watch him shift back to human. *What would that look like?* Speaking of which... "Jonah's Billy's younger brother, you said? He's not directly related to me, though, is he?" I bloody hoped not, but with my bad luck he probably would be.

Ruby frowned. "I don't think so, but we could check. Did you feel anything when you saw him?"

I tilted my head at her. "You mean other than terrified by the growling and all those sharp teeth?"

Ruby nodded. "That's normal. He couldn't control his shifter around you."

I laughed at that. "Yeah, he said that his shifter liked me. I thought the shifters hated us witches, and I'm three quarters witch." *And a quarter wolf shifter.* A fact I was still growing accustomed to thanks to Jonah showing me that wolves were beautiful, powerful creatures. And ones that the men could control, because he ran for the safety and wilds of the forest, and not toward another person in unchecked aggression.

Ruby took my hand. "Look, you may want to come back inside for a bit."

I pulled my cell phone out of my pocket and glanced at the time on the screen. "It's past four, Ruby. I really need to get home."

Ruby's lips twisted. "Um, you're going to need to hear this before you go, Bell."

"Why?" I pressed.

Ruby sighed.

I didn't budge. I needed to go, and I hated being late for my mom. She worried too much already. I'd been her everything for twenty-three years... "Are you sure this can't this wait until tomorrow? I agreed to come back in the morning and see Jonah for breakfast." Why? I had no idea. "Maybe I could pop in afterwards and we could catch up again? Let me know what your guys think of the painting and stuff."

Ruby pinched the bridge of her nose. "Bella, this is serious. The reason Jonah couldn't control his shifter around you, and he went all growly and strange..."

"Yeah?" That had been weird, but what was even more weird was that I wasn't scared of him at all at that moment. If anything, I'd found it intensely interesting.

"It's because you're his Fated mate."

CHAPTER 5
BELLA

My mouth dropped open. "I'm sorry, what?" *Impossible.* Surely, I would have known something as important as that instantly. "He can't be," I reasoned.

Ruby stared at me, then crossed her arms firmly over her chest before cocking an eyebrow at me. "Why not? Found another soul mate recently?"

"No! But..."

"But what?" she pushed.

I didn't have an answer because there was no answer that would have satisfied Ruby. I hadn't met anyone I'd thought was the one for me—including the man I'd just met. "But... he's Billy's cousin?" I asked, skeptical. That sounded somehow almost incestuous to me.

"And what's wrong with that? Jonah's cute! And I'll put money on that you're safe on the direct relation front."

Oh, he was more than cute. He was damn hot, with bright blue eyes and his funky, spiky hair. Although I hadn't seen him naked while he was shifting thanks to his clothes covering his human body, then the wolf appearing, I could see how lithe and strong, and sexy he must be underneath it all. I shook myself. "I know, but..."

Ruby sighed. "Obviously, you aren't feeling it all just yet. I mean, we're all different, but when I met Jackson, I knew straight away. He was the Alpha. But Jonah's a Beta, like Billy. So, maybe you just need to meet your Alpha as well?"

I gaped at her. "You've got to be kidding. I don't want more than one!"

Ruby laughed at me and rolled her eyes. "And why not?"

"Because..." *How could I say this without offending her?* "I wouldn't even know what to do with one man, Ruby, let alone three. I grew up with no brothers, no father, no uncles..."

"Neither did I, and I'm doing just fine with my boys, Bella."

"But we're different Ruby!" I huffed. "You're vibrant, and fun, and exciting. And I'm... well, *me*." I liked books and reading, and college for the learning angle, *not* the wild parties.

Ruby grinned at me. "Go on, go home, and have dinner with your mom. Just let me know if you find out anything more about our dads, or anything like that."

I grabbed my keys out of my bag and shot back. "You, too! Especially about the curse. That's the most interesting part of all this for me. I can only imagine how much power it took to curse this whole town."

"Shhh..." Ruby hissed at me. "Don't say that too loudly."

I slammed my hand over my mouth and whispered, "Sorry." It

probably wasn't the best idea to advertise to the wolf pack that we thought our old high warlock cursed them all. We needed proof before we said anything, and even better, a solution.

I waved to Ruby and headed to my car. Glancing back as I got in the door, I couldn't stop the strangely hysterical laughter that bubbled up in my throat. What had been a simple lunch with my friend had turned into something so much more. "What the hell was that?" I asked the car interior and shook my head.

When I arrived back at my mother's house, the home I'd grown up in, I couldn't shake the strange feeling that something had changed. But was it in me? Or something in my environment? I couldn't tell yet. But something beyond my control, something... truly magical was going on.

Once inside the house, I looked around as though I might discover something different. Perhaps sense the thing that had changed. But there was nothing new. Nothing at all. My house was still the same old mix of ordered chaos and the over-the-top injection of rainbow of colors that my mother enjoyed so much.

"Mom, I'm home," I called out.

"Hey Bella! How was your day?" She called back from the general direction of the kitchen.

"Ah, good thanks." *Overall, I suppose.* "Yours?" I put my bag on the floor and went straight for the bookshelf against the wall in the lounge room. I needed some answers. I had far too many questions at this point, which never sat well with me. And today, I wanted to know more about my future... and whether Jonah was in it. I didn't want to turn up to breakfast like an ignorant half-wit, tomorrow. Which, if I was honest, was probably half the reason I was feeling so unsettled.

I'd never been the kind of person who flew by the seat of their pants through life. I wanted to know what was going to happen today, tomorrow, next week, and next year if possible.

I grabbed a scrying book off the shelf, sat down on the couch cross-legged, and opened the massive tome. I'd looked in this book before, and I had a natural affinity with premonition spells—the ability to see into or predict the future. Unfortunately predicting the future and looking too far into your own future was frowned upon by the Coven. So, I tried not to do it too much.

"Dinners in the oven. It'll be about an hour," Mom said, walking into the room while drying her hands with a colorful towel. "What are you up to, sweetheart?" she asked curiously.

I flicked through the future-telling book and found a page I'd used before. It was a relatively easy spell, but it was limited in what you could see or feel. There was a lot of interpretation required, as well as a skilled witch's hand. I glanced up at my mom as she stared at me.

There was no point lying to her about what I was doing, or even trying to avoid the truth for that matter. For some reason, I couldn't lie to my mom. *None of us could.* Ruby and Tiffany, either. We were pretty sure our mothers had put a spell on us to conjure the truth at some point in our lives. It was subtle, but even now I could feel the warm pull at the back of my neck. *Pity the spell doesn't go both ways*, I mused.

"I had lunch at Ruby's new place, and met someone," I answered. "A wolf shifter named Jonah. Ruby said that I'm his mate. But I didn't feel the same way he did. Or, at least, I don't think I did. Honestly, I'm not even sure what I'm meant to feel."

My mom staggered forward as though she was unsteady or suddenly and inexplicably drunk.

"You okay?" I frowned, reaching out a steady hand toward her.

"Yeah, yeah. Fine, fine." Mom waved me away as she fell into the armchair opposite me. "What do you mean, he thinks you're his mate?"

I frowned at her. "I think it means that our soul mate spell worked on him, too. But I'm not sure."

My mom made a strange, choking noise.

I grimaced and looked back at her.

"Doesn't that mean anything to you, Bella?" she asked, her eyebrows high on her forehead as though she was surprised by my lack of reaction or excitement.

I shrugged. "I don't know, I guess." I slid to the floor, kneeling beside the coffee table and placed the book on the surface of the table. "I didn't feel the same things Ruby said he did. He was cute and everything, but I want to know for sure." There was no way I would even see him again unless I had a direction.

I'd always been quite good at scrying, though my mother would never allow me to look into the past, though I'd been tempted. What father-less daughter wouldn't want to know more about the past? Especially her mother's past, specifically.

Mom had always kept a priceless crystal ball in the middle of the table, sitting on a black ring pedestal to keep it from rolling away. Most of the time the crystal was a colorless, pretty orb. Nothing more than a New Age decoration to non-magical onlookers. But as I placed my hands on either side of its smooth, flawless surface and spoke the ancient language of the warlocks, the crystal ball began to swirl with smoke inside its depths, and flickers of bright green light appeared.

I mentally asked the scrying spell a question, then conjured up a feeling, an image of my future. *Was Jonah a part of my future? The answering call of the soul mate spell I'd cast last year with my friends?* The crystal orb glowed and hummed with a silent vibration. I couldn't see him in the mystical smoke, but the feeling I got was, *yes*, he was part of my future. But he wasn't the only one. There was more. More people. *More men.*

I dropped my hands away, letting the spell go. The smoke and intangible tendrils of magic faded away. I slumped. "Damn." Not the answer I'd been hoping for.

"What is it?" Mom asked.

I pushed myself back until I was resting against the couch and flicked the stray hair out of my face. "I have more than one soul mate, too."

My mom stilled, not uttering a sound.

I sighed and ran my fingers through the tangles of my long hair. I didn't want three mates like Ruby. *I didn't*. I hated being the center of attention! I looked up at my mother.

She was frozen in place and her eyes were wide, as though frightened.

"What?" I asked, my brows furrowing.

"I don't know quite what to say, Bell."

Well, at least that was honest.

"Me neither," I said, and sighed. "I'm not sure what to do."

She slid to the floor and joined me on the carpet, crossing her legs and sitting opposite me. She hadn't done that since I was a child.

I smiled at her, feeling like I was kindergarten age all over again and she was about to do a puzzle with me. "I'm impressed you can still sit like that," I said, indicating her crossed legs.

She grinned at me. "Yoga."

"Hmm…"

"Sweetheart, you know the soul mate spell is going to drag the man you're meant to love, meant to marry, out of hiding, don't you? I mean, it sounds like you're disappointed that Fate has sent you a person to love, which is exactly what you asked for."

"Oh, it's not that. It's just …" I stopped, not sure how to finish the sentence. *What was the problem?* I stared down at my lap and flicked a piece of fluff off my jeans. "I suppose I was hoping I'd get a few more years before they found me. I don't feel ready. Tiffany hasn't met her guy yet, or guys, and she's so much more ready than I am. Even Ruby was! I haven't finished college yet. I…"

"There's never a perfect time to meet the man you're supposed to fall in love with," Mom said softly. "When I met your father…"

I stared at her, watching the way she swallowed hard and glanced down at her multilayered, multicolored skirts. She'd never mentioned my father before, not like this. And certainly not in such soft tones.

"When I met your father," she repeated, "I was half-way through college, living at home with my parents. Very similar to you, actually."

"And what happened?" I asked, my heart aching with the need to know.

She chuckled. "I met him at a friend's party. These three hot boys showed up wearing leather jackets. On motorbikes. They were the coolest guys I'd ever seen."

The Manterri cousins. The shifters.

"What did my father look like?"

Mom smiled. "A lot like you. He has beautiful dark hair, perfect skin, and a stubborn jaw."

I ran my hand over my cheek, and cupped my chin, trying to imagine a man that looked like me. "And you knew he was for you? Did you experience the soul mate feeling?"

Mom nodded. "I didn't know it at the time. I honestly just thought he was cute. And I couldn't keep my eyes off him. But the more time we spent together; it became obvious that he was meant for me. And I for him." Mom fell silent.

A wave of pain washed over me. I reached out and grabbed her hand. "You still miss him?"

She smiled and for the first time in my whole life, I saw my mother cry real tears of sadness. Not like those from a movie, or the sort you get while chopping onions. Two large, single tears slid down her cheeks, and with them came a heavy cascade of true sadness.

She squeezed my hand. "I know you're scared, Bella, and I know I haven't set a good example for you in regards to marriage, or even a relationship. But to this day, I don't regret the time I spent with your father. I never will. Not even for a moment. So please, *please*, don't be afraid. Love and relationships are what life's all about. They're what make life worth living."

My voice hitched in my throat, but I swallowed the pain. "Even if they break your heart?" I asked quietly.

She nodded, genuine honesty in her gaze. "Even if they break your heart."

CHAPTER 6
JONAH

I drummed my fingers along the table at Milly's, nervous energy making every part of me practically vibrate.

"Can I get you anything, Jonah?" Tania, the waitress, and one of the last females to be born to our pack, asked as she smiled at me. She was twenty-three years old, like me, and had been mated since the day she turned eighteen. She'd been snaffled up by one of the older guys, desperate for a wife, after it became obvious that our pack was never going to have another daughter born to it again.

"No, thank you. I'm waiting for someone," I answered.

She quirked an eyebrow at me, curious as a cat. "Anyone I might know?"

There were only three unmated females of fertile age born in our pack, and they'd all frequented the beds of most of the guys in town. Not a problem if you liked that—but none of them were my style.

"Afraid not."

The bell above the door chimed. We turned as one toward the sound.

My heart began thumping madly in my chest when I laid eyes upon who'd arrived. I stared at Bella, my little witch mate, as she slid inside the loud café.

She cast her tentative gaze around the room.

Tania laughed and hurried over to where Bella stood, looking utterly beautiful but nervous as hell, in her blue denim jeans and bright purple tank.

I didn't bother trying to stop Tania from going up to her. Tania was a force of nature. And it was nice to just sit back and watch them for a minute.

Tania grinned and chatted amiably to Bella, then gestured to where I sat in the back.

Bella glanced my way, pursing her lips, and nodded.

Our gazes clashed in a heat that stole up my back and tingled along my neck like flickers of flame. My wolf leapt inside me in joy, instantly recognizing my mate in the beautiful young witch who walked toward me. *Calm the hell down*, I commanded.

I'd purposely run all afternoon yesterday, and all night, trying to tire my wolf out just so I could get some control today and be able to speak to her. But as I swallowed hard and forced my wolf down once again, I realized it was going to be way harder than I'd initially thought it would be.

Bella stepped up to my table.

I jumped to my feet, grinning at her. "Hey."

She bobbed her head a little, appearing shy. "Hi Jonah." She had beautiful long dark hair that shone in the light and fell across her shoulders as she stared at her shoes. When she finally managed to look up at me, despite the dark brown color of her eyes, purple magic swirled in their depths.

"Let's sit," I suggested, forcing myself not to touch her, though I desperately ached to haul her to my body, to kiss her, hold her, and keep her safe. I curled my fingers into tight fists, slid into the booth, and firmly placed both hands on my knees beneath the table. I didn't want her to see how hard I was fighting my wolf. *Relax! Stay down. You can run again later.* I cleared my throat with a rough cough. "Sit down." I gestured to the seat opposite me. "Please. Join me."

Bella nodded and slid onto the leather booth bench.

"You're human again," she observed.

The softness of her voice surprised me. Ruby was confident and charismatic, a proud witch who suited her three strong mates. Bella seemed shy and reserved in comparison. Very different from her friend. And I liked it. With a smile, I nodded. "I shifted back last night before bed."

She tilted her head as if studying me. "Is that normal?"

"Which bit?" *That I shifted? That I skipped meals? What?*

The edges of her lips lifted, and she stared intently at me. "That you would go all afternoon and evening in your wolf form?" she clarified.

I shook my head. "Not really. I can go weeks without shifting at all, and even then, I tend to only run for an hour, tops. I prefer being in my human form."

A lot of the other guys didn't—my brother Billy included—they felt much more confident in their wolf bodies.

"So, what happened yesterday?" she asked.

I raised my eyebrows. "Honestly?"

She became serious, her mouth flattening into an unforgiving straight line. "Always. Please."

Mental note: has issues about being lied to.

"Well, I transformed so quickly when I saw you yesterday, I was sort of hoping a good run would sort my wolf out and afford me more control today."

She smiled again. "And did it?"

I checked myself. I was more relaxed now that she was close to me and paying me attention. "Well, the words are flowing at least," I answered with a smile of my own.

"And your wolf?" she asked, genuinely interested.

I grinned. "He's close to the surface, but I've got a handle on him."

She slid her hands over the table, moving slightly closer. "And is it true that you have complete control over your wolf? That your brain functions as though you were still human?"

Tania walked up and handed us some menus, temporarily interrupting our conversation. "You two ready to order?"

Bella scanned the menu quickly, then looked to me. "Any suggestions?"

"They make the best cooked breakfast around. And hamburgers."

Bella smiled at Tania and handed back the menu. "Eggs benedict and a chocolate milkshake, please."

Tania glanced at me.

"The usual, please, Tania."

She smiled briefly and headed off.

Bella looked at me. "So, you eat here often?"

I laughed. "It's the only eatery in town and I like a cooked breakfast."

"Fair enough," Bella said, and we lapsed into comfortable silence. Then my little mate looked up, her bright eyes sharp with interest.

"What do you do, Jonah?"

"I'm a brick layer," I said, shrugging. I wasn't one of those guys who defined themselves by what they did for a crust. It made me money, and it helped the community, but it wasn't my life. "It's physical work, and early mornings, but I like it."

She grinned shyly. "The exercise must be good, too?"

"How about you?" I countered.

She smiled shyly. "I'm actually at college at the moment, finishing up my degree in teaching."

I couldn't help myself. I grinned. "I would have loved to have had a teacher who looked like you back in high school."

Her cheeks turned a pretty pink color, then she glanced down at the table. "Thanks, but I'd prefer to teach at an elementary school. I like the little ones."

The bell above the door rang, as it had been all morning with people coming in and going out, but this time the sound caught my attention.

I glanced up as my oldest brother Thomas walked in.

"Hey, Jonah!" he called out.

I raised my hand to wave and sighed at the interruption. I should have assumed we'd be spotted.

Bella froze. Then she shivered, and turned around slowly, staring at the door of the café where Thomas, and his best friend Elliot, stood.

The two guys stared at my mate.

She stared right back. "Who are they?" she whispered, the desire in her voice impossible to ignore.

Damn it. I swallowed my need to question her about who she meant, and what she was feeling. It was painfully obvious. Her pupils were dilated, and her gaze was hungry. I could literally see the desire for them on her face, and their attraction for her was written all over theirs. It was all there. The attraction, the sizzle, the need.

My brother and his best friend stumbled forward, toward us. They didn't take their eyes off Bella.

I stood up, ready to direct them to the door the moment they needed to shift, which if they were her mate, they'd likely need to. *Shit. I was hoping I was her only one.*

Thomas began to say, "Jonah... ah..." But words failed him, and his throat worked as he swallowed hard.

I moved over to stand in front of my mate.

She sat still on the bench seat, just staring up at the two Alpha males in front of us.

I gestured to her by way of introduction. "This is Bella. She's one of Ruby's friends."

"She's a witch?" Elliot asked, shock evident in his tone.

I narrowed my eyes at them. "And she's my mate, though from the looks of you guys..."

Thomas visibly shook.

Elliot's eyes were practically popping out of his head.

"Your *what?*" Elliot asked as a low growl emerged.

Bella pushed herself to her feet.

I moved toward her protectively, shielding her.

She pressed into my side and grabbed onto my arm.

My wolf surged inside of me, pleasure zinging along my skin at her touch.

Bella gasped.

And I found myself hoping that she felt the same thing.

"What's wrong with them?" she hissed quietly at me.

I grinned, though part of me was devastated. Bella had more than one mate. Just like Ruby. *Pull yourself together, man. If Billy can be happy in a pack of three men sharing one woman, so can you.* I smiled down at her. "Same as what was up with me yesterday."

Bella's eyes widened, then she bit her lip. She knew what I meant, though I wasn't sure how she felt about it. At that moment, she seemed a little scared.

I turned to my brother and Elliot, both of whose eyes had shifted to those of their inner wolves.

"Go shift and run. It helps. I'll fill you both in later."

"But..." Tommy tried to talk, but he was shaking too much to get anything more out.

I sighed heavily. "Trust me on this. Go run. I'll catch up with you guys later." When they didn't move, I turned to my beautiful witch. "Tell them you're not going anywhere. I think they're afraid you'll leave, and they'll lose you."

Both men made strangled, grunting noises. They probably didn't like me revealing such things so openly, but she liked the truth, so she was getting the truth.

She bit her lip. "Well, I do have classes after lunch, but I could come back around dinner time?"

"Perfect," I said, overriding any sort of rejection of the plan the other two guys might have had in mind. "You'll meet us back here tonight then, yeah?"

"Yes." She swallowed hard, her gaze roving over the two Alphas, before returning to me. "Sixish?"

"Done." I turned back to the other two. "Now, go. Before you shift and make a mess of the diner. Tania won't be impressed."

Elliot grabbed onto Tommy's arm and pulled hard. "Let's go," he managed to say, though it came out all garbled and weird.

My brother planted his feet, not wanting to move, fighting against his friend.

But Elliot tugged at him harder, practically wrestling him almost all the way to the door.

I wrapped my arm around Bella's shoulders.

Her small body trembling beneath mine.

"Go. It's all good," I assured them.

The two guys stared at us, then they both fell out the front doors and shifted into their massive white wolf forms.

Bella's jaw dropped as she stared after them through the glass. "They're white, too," she whispered.

"Yeah." I didn't really get what that had to do with anything.

My mate shivered even more in response.

I tugged her back into the booth with me and wrapped my arms around her. "Now, tell me what you're feeling, because I want you to feel safe here." I expected words. I expected laughter. I certainly didn't expect what came next.

Tears rolled down her cheeks and she cuddled into my chest and sobbed as though her very heart was breaking.

Shit. What the hell did I do now?

CHAPTER 7
BELLA

No matter what I did, I couldn't stop shaking or crying. I felt utterly ridiculous.

But Jonah held me, and rocked me, and told me everything was going to be okay.

There was no choice but to go with the torrent of emotions buffering my senses, cuddle into the guy offering me a shoulder to cry on and wait out the storm. Finally, after it felt like my throat would break from the sobbing, the tantalizing aroma of eggs and bacon reached me through the haze of my pain, and I realized the waitress was serving our food.

"Thanks, Tania," Jonah said over my head.

"Is she okay?" Tania whispered.

I nodded, wiping my face. "Sorry. I'm okay."

Tania pressed some napkins into my hand, and I pulled away from Jonah's hot body—both the temperature and his rock-hard muscles.

"Sorry," I said again, seeing all the tear stains I'd left behind on his shirt. "I'll fix that." I waved my hand and got rid of all the evidence of my emotional trauma from his shirt. I didn't try and fix myself up. I knew my face was red and blotchy, but there was no point if I was just going to burst into tears again, which at this point, it felt like I was definitely going to.

"Have something to eat," Tania said. "You'll feel better." She walked away to serve another table, leaving me with one of my wolf mates.

One of three. I hung my head. "Three. I don't want three."

"Three what?" Jonah asked, picking up his knife and fork. "There's three rashers of bacon and three sausages if you want some of mine?"

Three sausages... Oh, my God. I should have cried again, but instead I burst out laughing, snorting so inelegantly I had to slam my hand over my mouth to stop the spit and snot flying across the table. I almost died. Okay, so maybe I needed a little magical clean up. I waved my hand over my face, drying my eyes and nose. I blinked at Jonah.

He was cutting and eating and drinking like a machine.

"Hungry?" I asked rhetorically.

He nodded. "Always. How about you?"

I stared down at my breakfast, and even though it looked and smelled amazing I was not hungry at all anymore. But I would be later, so I picked up my milkshake and took a long draw, filling my mouth with the icy cold drink and swallowing hard.

Three. I had *three.* That was three men. Three hearts to love. Three penises to... satisfy. Three different personalities to mesh with mine. This was going to be impossible. *Impossible!* My eyes began to burn with tears again.

Jonah reached across the table and squeezed my arm. "Hey, hey. It's okay. Whatever's upsetting you, I'm sure we can fix it."

I lifted my gaze to his. "I somehow doubt it."

"Try me."

I exhaled sharply. "I don't want three mates."

Jonah's eyes widened, then he grinned. "Sounds good to me. I can keep you all to myself. How about we run off together? Just you and me."

I opened my mouth to agree, but the words got so stuck in my throat and it felt like someone had squeezed my larynx shut or like someone had rubbed it raw with sandpaper. I swallowed furiously, then took another long sip of my milkshake through the straw. I tried to speak again, but this time my heart physically ached. My ribs squeezed and deep inside my chest, I hurt. I couldn't say it. I couldn't agree. It's like my entire body rebelled at the idea of abandoning my other two mates. I slumped. "I don't think that's a possibility."

Jonah sighed. "Yeah, I know... or at least, I assume that's the case."

"What do you mean?" I asked, finding my voice more easily now.

He scooped some of his eggs onto his fork, then stuffed them in his mouth. "Well, I kind of hoped I'd be your only mate, even though Ruby has three. After all, those four are the first of their kind, so none of us expected the pattern to repeat."

I nodded, slightly amused that Jonah had jumped straight to that conclusion.

"So, you think we're Fated too?" I asked.

He nodded. "There's no denying my wolf's response to you. What about you? How do you feel about me?"

I shivered, wanting to be honest with him. "I didn't feel as much yesterday as I thought I should, but when I touched you just before..."

"Yes?" he prompted, grinning madly.

"Did you feel it too?" I asked tentatively. "That... tingle?" The moment I'd reached for him, more in fear than anything else, my breath had been sucked from my lungs and my core had tightened and pulsed with longing. I'd never felt anything like it before in my life. I wanted to melt into his arms, press my lips to his bare neck, and taste him. Then the intensity of the other two had overwhelmed me. Distracted me from the moment.

"I felt *a lot* more than that." He grinned, then sobered. "Is that why you're upset? Because you felt the same thing for Tommy and Elliot?"

I swallowed hard, my stomach twisting. "Is that their names?" I hated that I could feel so much for men whose names I didn't even know.

Jonah nodded. "They're both Alphas. And Tommy's my older brother."

My mouth dropped open and a single word fell from my lips. "No."

"No, what?"

"I can't handle two Alphas!" I grabbed my head in my hands and squeezed my temples. I couldn't handle one Alpha male! Let alone the brother thing. I couldn't even think about that bit. "Oh, my God. This is such a mess. Okay. All right, let's run away." The moment I said the words, pain struck me in the chest like a hot iron. I pressed a hand to my sternum. "Stop that," I told myself, instantly frustrated.

Jonah laughed. "Stop what?"

I swallowed hard, picking up my knife and fork. *Maybe I was just hungry and it was heartburn?* "Every time I even try and talk about leaving the other two, my chest caves in and it feels like I'm going to die. It hurts." I stabbed my poached eggs, the yellow yolk running over my muffins and smoked salmon.

"Sounds like your body doesn't want you giving them up," Jonah said quietly, and this time a wave of sadness radiated from him.

"I'm sorry," I said, though I had no control over my response. "I don't want three mates, but it seems I have no choice." There was absolutely no denying the way I was attracted to them, though. When Tommy and Elliot had walked into the café, I'd shivered all over, feeling the magic—the draw of them from our soul mates spell. I'd wanted to throw myself into their arms... until they started growling and stiffening up as though they were angry at me.

"So that's why you're upset? You'd prefer just one partner?"

The hopeful expression on Jonah's face made my heart ache in an altogether different way. I didn't want to give him false hope. He seemed like such a sweet, good guy. Unfortunately, there seemed to be a feisty, hot female lying dormant inside of me. And she wanted, no, needed Elliot and Tommy too. "I've always thought I'd have one soul mate. A husband." I jabbed absently at my breakfast with my knife again. "But it looks like Fate has a different plan for me."

There was no arguing with that.

"Billy said that Ruby and her friends cast a soul mate spell. Was that you?" Jonah asked, shoveling the last of his greasy, awesome breakfast into his mouth.

I nodded. "To be honest, I wasn't that interested in conducting the spell, but Ruby and Tiffany talked me into it. At the time, I felt like I couldn't let them down. Those girls have always been like sisters to me."

He cocked his head. "Why weren't you?"

I glanced down. "Because there was a warning attached to the spell. It said there would be a payment taken for a successful result."

"A payment?"

I nodded. "It didn't say what sort, and considering how unwell Ruby has been since after Halloween, the spell obviously took its pound of flesh from her."

"At least she has her three guys now," Jonah said with a shrug, as though that was enough of a reward for enduring life possibly magicless.

I opened my mouth, then thought better of what I was about to say. "Yeah, well Ruby's happy, I guess." And she was. She'd outright said she'd be happy to pay the cost of finding her mates.

"And you're worried about what you'll lose?" Jonah asked, pushing his plate away and leaning back against the booth. As he did, he glanced at me and the sunlight caught the blue in his eyes, making them sparkle.

My breath caught in my throat. *Damn*, he was beautiful. I reached across the space between us and touched him, wanting to feel his skin beneath my fingers. I ran my hand down his forearm until I could intertwine my fingers with his.

He shivered and goosebumps prickled his skin.

"Does that feel good for you too?" I asked.

He gave me a wolf-like smile, all teeth and flashy grin. "If I didn't know that my brother would kill me for seducing you, I'd throw you over my shoulder and take you back to my place right now."

The smile fell from my face, and I pulled my hand back.

He reached out in spite of my sudden withdrawal and took my hand in his, interlacing our fingers.

Warm tendrils of heat curled in my belly. *Whoa. Yes, Jonah is my soul mate. This attraction is intense.*

"Hey. Chill. I was just joking," Jonah said, squeezing my hand gently. "I'm not a pushy guy, at all, I promise. We can sit here and talk all year if you like. Though I might try to steal a kiss or two." He winked with a charming smile.

I swallowed hard and licked my dry lips.

"What's wrong?"

How could I tell a guy that at twenty-two, I'd never been kissed? "Well, I..." I flicked my hair over my shoulder and looked him straight in the eye. If I couldn't tell Jonah, I didn't have a hope in hell of telling the other two. I opened my mouth to tell him, but the words simply failed me.

I decided to do something completely out of character for me and show him what I meant. After all, they said that actions speak louder than words. I leaned forward, tilted my chin up, and reached for his face—to pull him to me. Surely, he'd feel my inexperience when I gave him the world's worst kiss imaginable?

Jonah's eyes went wide, and I was pretty sure I saw a flash of yellow in his otherwise blue irises, before he surged forward to kiss me.

I moaned at the suddenness of it all, the pressure.

Then his lips softened, and he cupped my cheek.

I sighed, expecting him to back away.

Instead, he deepened the kiss, sweeping his tongue out to brush against the seam of my lips.

I opened to him and he tasted the inside of my mouth. Another moan erupted from my throat as I tried to get closer to him, feeling awkward in the booth, all squashed and sideways.

A soft growl rolled through Jonah's throat as I lifted my tongue to tangle with his. He tasted of heat and lust.

As desire curled through my belly, blazing to life like a wildfire, I realized I'd been kidding myself if I thought for even a moment that I wasn't really attracted to this guy. I was. Completely. If the table hadn't been in my way, I would have swung my leg over his waist and straddled him, just to get closer to his heat. To the *heart* of him.

He broke away, panting hard. "If you were trying to convince me *not* to seduce you, there are more convincing ways." He grinned.

My gaze dropped straight to his mouth. I lifted my hand tentatively and pressed my fingers to his lips. My mouth throbbed with blood and feel of Jonah's possession.

Jonah groaned and leaned close, his hot breath sweeping against my ear. "Are you sure you don't wanna go back to my place for a bit?"

God, I wanted to. I ached to find out more about the physical love side of this thing. But something stopped me. "Can I tell you one thing before we go anywhere?"

He pulled back from whispering in my ear to grin down at me. "Of course. What is it?"

"I'm a..." I swallowed hard. *Virgin* was such a strange word to say out loud, so I opted for a different choice of words. "I've never had sex with anyone before." The idea of having sex with all three of my supposed 'mates' was terrifying.

Jonah pulled a bit further back, his mouth dropping open in shock or awe, or perhaps both. "Are you serious, Bella?"

"Of course, I am. That's hardly something to lie about."

He grabbed my face in his hands so suddenly I gasped. The he started kissing me all over again, fast, intense, and all-consuming.

I closed my eyes and willingly went along for the dizzying, heady ride. Obviously my being a hopeless virgin wasn't a turn-off for this guy. Hopefully, Elliot and Tommy would feel the same way—though a part of me knew they wouldn't.

CHAPTER 8
TOMMY

E lliot and I ran until we were exhausted, then ran some more. Through the forest and past the town. When I was finally aching in every joint and all four paws, Elliot and I turned around and ran all the way back to our pack.

If that didn't wear out my wolf long enough to give me some breathing room to speak to Bella, I didn't know what would.

When we finally got back to town, we went straight for our shack, the small two-bedroom house Elliot and I shared.

I ran for the back door and closed my eyes, letting go of my wolf so that I could shift back to my human form. My back legs elongated, and I lost my black and white vision so that I could see in color once again. It was still afternoon judging by the look of where the golden sun hung suspended in the sky.

Elliot shifted next to me and slowly stretched up to his full height.

I grinned at him. "We found our mate."

Elliot didn't smile back. "You really think she has two Alpha mates?"

I shrugged. "Why? You willing to give her up?"

Elliot growled, low and threatening.

Surprised by his aggression, I glared at him. "Back the fuck up. I was joking." I pushed at our back door, already annoyed. Storming into our kitchen, I pulled some energy drinks out of the fridge. I threw one to Elliot, then opened one for myself.

A lot of people had said that two Alphas couldn't be as close as we'd always been. Best friends. Living together. But we'd always made it work, until now.

"Listen," I said, "she's my mate. I know it in my bones. All the signs are there. The instant attraction. The scent of her drives me wild. And of course, my total loss of control when it came to my shifter." I stared at Elliot, waiting for him to say something. Anything.

All he did was grunt. "Yeah, and...?"

For fuck's sake... seriously? I grabbed my sports drink, chugged down the full bottle, then threw it toward the recycling. "So, did you feel the same thing? Is she your mate as well? Or did I read you all wrong when I saw you shaking like a damn leaf at Milly's?" I glared at him.

And he glared back.

I probably shouldn't have poked him about his reaction to our mate, but *hell*, he was being a dick about all of this.

Elliot didn't deign to answer me. He just stormed off toward the bathroom. "I'm going to have a shower."

I glanced at the time. "It's five already, so I'll be heading off to Milly's in forty-five. You coming?"

Elliot just slammed the bathroom door behind him.

"Wanker," I muttered under my breath with a sigh. I leaned back against the counter and ran my hands through my hair. Jeez. I'd never imagined my mate could be so beautiful or so young. And even in all my craziest dreams I certainly never would have guessed she'd be a witch. I laughed and shook my head. "Billy's going to give me bloody hell for this." I'd teased my younger brother for weeks over his mate, Ruby, being a witch. I had it coming now!

I headed upstairs to my own private bathroom to have a shower and a shave. I didn't care if my mate was a dark-haired witch. Or that she was younger than my youngest brother, which made her at least ten years my junior. She was beautiful. And she was mine.

Since I'd all but given up any hope of being mated, and having a family, this felt like a literal dream come true. If I had to share her, then so be it—my inner Alpha be damned. If Billy could do it, and if an Alpha like Jackson could too, so could I. But whether Elliot could share her with us? Well, that was a question I didn't know the answer to.

ONCE I WAS DRESSED in my best jeans and favorite black shirt, I headed downstairs.

Elliot was nowhere to be seen. He'd obviously decided he didn't want to see Bella again.

That was fine by me. If he wanted to give Fate the big middle finger, so be it. But I damn well wasn't going to. This was the opportunity of a lifetime. Everything I'd ever wanted, albeit a little different than I envisaged. I grabbed my cell phone and wallet and headed out the door. Elliot wasn't a child, and I wasn't his bloody mother. If he didn't want to see our mate again, then that was on him. It was his life, not mine. I wouldn't be the one living with regret.

Personally, I thought it was pretty ridiculous to leave her to Jonah and me, but I'd never bothered to try and figure out Elliot or his moods before. Then again, I'd never really cared before that he was a grumpy bastard. It didn't affect me when I was just his best friend. But as his co-mate, or whatever we wanted to call this new relationship dynamic we found ourselves in, it might become an issue that needed to be resolved in future.

I walked the two blocks over to the main drag, that only consisted of four shops, then stopped dead. There she was. I opened my mouth, forcing myself to breathe as my heart hammered like a drum in my chest. *God, she's an angel.*

Bella stepped out of her little car and looked around as though she was lost. Her eyes were big and her shoulders slumped.

I wanted nothing more than to go over there and kiss her worries away.

She bit her lip like she was nervous, and the breeze ruffled her long dark hair around her, making her appear even more sensual and inviting. She tucked the loose strands behind her ear, seemingly uncertain of what to do next.

My heart squeezed tight at just how right this all felt. And then I was walking across the street before I'd even decided to move. I stepped around a passing truck and grinned.

My mate whirled around to stare at me wide-eyed like a deer caught in headlights, as though she'd heard me approaching—which was almost impossible. She must have *felt* me somehow, as I moved like most shifters did—with perfect stealth.

"Hey," I managed to say, though my wolf rose within me like I hadn't run him for eight hours today. *Calm down.* I swallowed hard, willing my human self to stay attentive and strong. "We didn't officially meet this morning. I'm Tommy." I extended my hand, wanting to touch her.

She stared up at me with those dark, beautiful eyes.

All I wanted to do was reach for her so I could cup her face and press my lips against hers in a deep, possessive kiss. Then I noticed the swirl of purple, the magic deep within her and I decided that sweeping her up into a kiss, moments after officially meeting my witch mate, might not be the smartest move of my life. I didn't want to magically end up on my ass.

"I'm Bella," she said and reached for my hand.

I shook her hand and the second our skin touched everything inside me exploded with rapture. I gasped, gripping her fingers tighter to capture and hold onto the feeling.

She began to crumple.

I let go of her hand and swept her up into my arms before her head hit the concrete. "Whoa. I've got you."

She put her head on my chest and her hand on my neck. She panted as though she'd run a mile.

My skin tingled from head to toe in a similar way to what I feel before I shift. With knowledge. With power. With intense awareness. I shivered, suppressing the growl that rose in my throat. "Are you okay?" I asked her, not able to see her face.

She glanced down, her hair falling over her cheek. "Yeah, I'm okay. But that was a bit intense. Can we go maybe inside?"

People walking by looked at us strangely. It was a small town; everyone knew everyone. Which meant Bella stood out like a bulldog's balls, and the fact I was holding her in my arms was a strong testament as to my commitment to her.

"Sure. Let's go." I hoisted her up higher in my arms and made for the front door.

A heavy hand landed on my shoulder, stopping me in my tracks. "What happened to her?"

I turned to see Elliot frowning down at me. "Get the door, would you?" I said tersely.

Elliot glared at me but grabbed the handle and held open the door open for us.

"Couldn't stay away, huh?" I threw over my shoulder, unable to resist.

Elliot growled.

Bella shivered in my arms.

I grimaced. "You're scaring her. If you're gonna be like that, you can fuck right off."

Elliot's eyebrows drew together as he glared pure fire at me.

I could see he was about to spit back at me.

Bella's hand reached out for him unexpectedly. She touched his skin and squeezed his arm with need. "Don't go," she said. Two of the sweetest words I'd ever heard. My best friend didn't stand a chance against her.

Elliot's face changed from one of intense anger to one of complete passive helplessness. He swallowed hard, his throat working, then he nodded. "Okay."

I rolled my eyes. I didn't think she'd cast an actual spell on him, but she may as well have.

Jonah came rushing up from the back of the eatery. "What happened? Bella? Are you okay?" He cupped Bella's face and ran his hand all over her.

Every part of me wanted to scream at him that he needed to back off. But I didn't need to say anything.

Jonah seemed to get the message as he locked eyes with me, froze, then began to back away. "I've got a booth," he offered. "Come sit in the back, with me." He turned on his heel and walked away at pace.

I shared a glance with Elliot. I knew exactly what he was thinking. Were we going to have to put up with living with my little brother for the rest of our lives? *Oh fuck, heaven help us.* And him. I walked ten or so feet to where Jonah had slid into our booth.

Bella wiggled in my arms. "Um, you can put me down now."

I didn't want to, but what sort of man didn't put a woman down when she asked? *A sicko. So, put her down.* I tilted forward and let Bella slide out of my arms and to her feet.

She shuffled around the table and sat with Jonah, pressing right up against him. Hip to hip. Shoulder to shoulder.

I glanced over at Elliot. *Oh, crap.*

We were Alphas.

Jonah was a Beta.

Bella shouldn't be cuddling up to him like that. It went against traditional pack politics and the expected, normal female behavior. And yet our mate seemed to know him, and at the moment, she also seemed to like him better than she did us.

Acknowledging that apparent fact felt like trying to swallow a throatful of sawdust. I shuffled over the seat. "Thanks for coming back tonight, Bella. I know this morning must have been strange for you," I said to break the tension.

Elliot slid into the booth beside me, managing to not touch me despite the fact that we barely fit together in the seat.

She smiled. "It's okay. I know we probably have a lot to talk about."

"Yes, I suppose we do."

Her gaze slid up to Jonah, then across the table to stare at us. She took a deep breath, then began what sounded like a rehearsed speech. "I have to be honest with you guys, here. I'm not sure I'm cut out to deal with three mates. Honestly, I doubt I'll be a good mate for one of you, let alone all three, but if you want me…"

"I want you," Jonah said straight away, his hand sliding over hers, where she rested her hand on the tabletop. "We'll work it out, somehow. I'm sure. We'll just take it one day at a time."

Bella's gaze flicked up to mine.

I opened my mouth to say the same thing. But the only 'words' that came out were garbled growls of anger.

Bella turned to Elliot, her gaze hopeful, but he'd already slid out of the booth and was sauntering toward the exit.

Damn it. I swallowed hard and forced myself to focus, to speak bloody coherent words. "I want you, Bella."

An answering smile trembled on her lips. "Thank you, Tommy. But why do I feel like my heart just marched out on me?" she asked, watching after the other Alpha.

Elliot threw open the door to Milly's and left.

I sighed. Part of me had hoped that having two Alphas in this pack was going to be a mistake. But that was selfish, because from the look on Bella's face, the only mistake that had been made, was that we'd let the dickhead walk out the door in the first place.

CHAPTER 9

ELLIOT

Of all the stupid, fucking things to do. Anger surged through me at a phenomenal rate of knots. I couldn't stop the feeling. It was like the tide, or the moon. Gravity even! It was inevitable. My hands clenched by my side and my vision flashed from wolf to human. The urge to scream—to howl to the moon—was so strong that my throat ached.

I stormed down the street, my wolf rising into the outer edges of my subconscious. What was I going to do? My mate was here. *My mate!* I should be at Milly's still wooing her and seducing her, before I dragged her back to my bed to make love to her for so long, and so well, that she'd never leave me. Never even consider looking at another man. Except, this mate, my mate... *would*. No matter what I did. And she *always* would.

She had two other male mates. I'd never be able to convince her that I was good enough to be her one and only mate. Jonah and Tommy would always be there. In our life. In our... bed. A sick, twisted smile screwed up my face. *Tommy*. Of all people. I loved the guy. Truly. Like a brother. Even more than my own damn brothers, in fact.

I'd reconciled myself to the fact that I'd probably live with him for the rest of my life, if I couldn't find a mate. But I didn't want to share a woman with him! I didn't want to see him naked and fucking her. I shuddered. The very thought of watching my best friend fucking my mate almost made me lose it. A growl rumbled in my chest. My shifter called to burst free. To run. To get away from the pain, the anxiety, and the jealousy.

But one thing held me back, a single tendril of logic that my wolf couldn't fight. Despite the fact she looked at least ten years younger than me, and she was a witch—one of those that we had been taught to fear, to hate—she was here. In the pack grounds. And she wanted me! That is if I read her touch and her looks correctly.

I reached the edge of town, and ahead of me was a winding gravel road that would take me to the highway. My wolf itched to shift and run, to escape from the unpleasantness that came with being human. With being *me*. But as I stared down the road out of town, I realized I couldn't go. I didn't want to run away from my mate. I wanted to look at her. Touch her. Hear her voice. Protect her.

I turned back around and stared down the main street of our town. Could I do it? Share my mate? Probably not. Jonah would submit to me if it came to a fight between the three of us. But Tommy? A grudging respect swept through me at the thought of my best friend. *Hell no, he'd never submit.* Not on his life.

Although I was taller and heavier, Tommy had cunning and speed on his side, attributes that would serve our mate well if she needed to be protected. As that thought snaked through my consciousness, I sighed and began to amble back to Milly's.

Thinking about what my mate needed, and wanted, should be my top priority. My everything. It was where my parents' marriage had failed. They'd both been too selfish, only looking after their own needs. They'd had one of the only failed matings in the long history of our pack.

I groaned as I trudged forward, running two hands through my hair and squeezing my head with my palms like I was being held in a vice. I had both of their genetics. Selfishness was literally in my blood. Why else would I feel this way? And yet Tommy was quite happy to share with Jonah? Share a mate. A woman. *Her pussy.* I shuddered at the thought, and yet my feet kept dragging me back the way I'd come.

Jonah stood at the edge of the street staring at me.

I groaned aloud. Had the young pup seriously come after me? I didn't see Bella or Tommy anywhere else. I stopped where I was, about half a block away.

Jonah waited for a car to drive past, then jogged over the road toward me.

I crossed my arms over my chest. "Come to find me?"

He grinned at me, undeterred by my size or strength. I'd always admired the kid for that.

"Coming back to us because you realized you made a mistake?" he countered.

I growled at him.

He laughed. "Yeah, I figured as much. Are you going to come back? Bella's been saying she wants to go home, but I don't think she really wants to. It's more that she doesn't feel welcome."

He didn't say anything about the fact that *I* was the reason she felt so unwelcome, but I got the message loud and clear. "Okay," I said. "Let's go." I followed the kid back to Milly's to see Bella arguing with Tommy. I frowned and dashed over to them. "What's going on?"

They turned to look at me and Bella's eyes were full of tears.

I reached for her, and she came into my arms. I held her close, her face pressed tightly against my chest. I rested my chin on her head. She was the perfect height for me. A wave of undeniable longing passed over me, almost stealing my breath away. I wrapped my arms around her and just held her. *Oh, my God. I'm never going to let this woman go.* I forced my eyes open, even though I wanted to simply remain there and rock her forever. "What's going on?" I repeated.

Tommy shrugged. "She wants to go home. I was just trying to get her to stay for dinner."

Bella lifted her head and looked up at me, her heart in her eyes. "I really want to go. Can you take please me?"

I nodded. There was no way I could deny her. "If she wants to go, I'll drive her." I pulled back, though a wave of cold moved in the moment she stepped away from me.

"We'll all go," Tommy said.

"*No.*" The word shot out of me so fast I couldn't stop it. I glanced at Bella with a grimace of half-hearted apology. "Would you be okay with me driving you?"

She stared at me a second, then nodded. "Yes. I think we need to chat."

Yeah, we probably did. I grinned at her. "You could probably blast me out of the car if I do or say anything you don't like, right?"

She smiled slowly through her tears. "I could blast you out of this diner if I wanted to, but I'm not afraid of you Elliot."

My mouth dropped open. She looked sweet, innocent, and delicate, but there was steel in the petals of this flower. I liked it. A lot.

She turned toward the other two, who were veritably pouting. "I'll be back here tomorrow, with my mom, for Thanksgiving. We're having lunch over at Ruby's house."

Tommy went to say something.

Jonah put a hand out and stopped him, surprisingly commanding his silence. "We'll see you then."

I nodded at my fellow co-mates and took Bella's hand, a sizzle of awareness shooting up my arm. I swallowed the moan that rose in me with difficulty.

We exited through the front door.

I glanced left and right. I'd lived here my whole life, and yet in this moment, with my mate's hand in mine, all I could feel buzzing through my veins was my need to protect her. As if danger might come from anywhere.

"Where's your car?" Bella asked me.

"It's back at my place. You okay to walk a few blocks? It's not far."

She nodded. "I'd like that actually. I need to clear my head."

I intertwined our fingers so she couldn't go anywhere. "This way."

We walked across the road, down to the end of the shops, then turned right off the main street, heading toward my place.

"It's only another block or so," I told her, relieved that my wolf seemed to have quietened since walking with her. Or maybe it was the touch of Bella's skin on mine. But there was something substantial holding me anchored in my human form.

"Okay."

We strolled the rest of the way in silence, though I got the feeling she wanted to say something but wasn't ready. Not yet anyway.

We arrived at my place, and I tugged her toward my truck. "I don't assume you want to see inside?" I asked, indicating the house, and then fished my car keys from my pocket.

Bella turned toward the small two-bedroom house Tommy and I had built about five years ago, when both of us had realized we couldn't live with anyone else, and our fated mates were nowhere to be found. "Who lives here with you?" she asked.

"Just Tommy and me."

She turned again to stare at me, her eyebrows drawn down in a frown, as though confused. "You two live together?"

"Yeah. Why?"

"Because... I don't know. I guess I kind of got a strange, competitive vibe from the two of you."

I laughed. She read us well, which would hold her in good stead for the future. I leaned against my truck and crossed my arms over my chest. "We have an insane rivalry for best friends. But that's what kind of makes us work. You want to see inside?" I asked again.

She raised an eyebrow at me. "I wouldn't mind, but you seem ready to go, already. What's wrong? Haven't cleaned the place up in a while?"

I chuckled and shook my head. "We don't clean up. We're bachelors—or were," I corrected.

"Then what's the problem?" she asked.

How honest could I be with a woman like this? I could smell the innocence on her—something else that was driving my wolf absolutely insane!

I cocked my head to the side and stared at her. "The problem is that if I get you within ten feet of a bed, you're not going to stay vertical for very long."

She yelped and practically ran over to the car, her dark hair whipping behind her.

Yep. Far too innocent for me.

She hustled around to the passenger side of the car.

I stared over the top of the cabin. "Are you as innocent as you smell?"

"As I *smell?*" she asked, her voice going all squeaky as though she was offended or shocked by the question.

I nodded. Of course, there was one good way to tell: sink my cock into her and see how tightly she squeezed me. I shook the thought off. "Well?" I repeated.

"Well, what?"

"Are you a virgin?" *Please, please, don't be a virgin. I'm not sure if I have the patience, or control for that.*

Her eyes went strangely wide, then she nodded.

Damn it. I groaned. "Get in the car before I make a fool out of us both."

She jumped into the truck.

I closed my eyes and threw back my head. If I made a list of everything I didn't want in a mate, Bella was practically the epitome of it. Too sweet. Too young. A witch, for heaven's sake. And of all things? A fucking... virgin! How the hell was she ever going to handle someone like me?

I threw myself into the car and turned on the engine. There was one thing for certain though. I might fear her ability to handle my sex drive and strength, but my wolf loved the idea that she'd never been taken. I would be her first. I'd make sure of it. Perhaps not her only. Perhaps not her last. But I would stamp my ownership on this little witch so that she'd never leave me. She'd never want for anything while I was around.

If I had to share her with my co-mates, then so be it. But even as the thought spun around in my head, my stomach tightened like I'd taken a punch to the gut and my heart sank. This wasn't what I wanted. Not at all.

CHAPTER 10

BELLA

I wrapped my arms around myself, suddenly freezing. Anxiety skittered along my nerves like sparks along live wire. I was about ready to fling my magic around the car and transport myself back home. But as I bit my lip and glanced over at the guy filling the car beside me with his massive bulk, and obvious resentment, I couldn't do it.

Running away from him would be the worst mistake of my life. I knew it. I could feel it in every premonition, and magical bone in my body. The same way I knew my mother regretted nothing more than leaving my father alone long enough for whatever had happened to happen.

There was a difference in our situations, obviously, but I was drawn to this huge hulking Alpha more than anyone. *Why?* I had no idea. He was a mystery. That was for certain. "Are you angry at me?" I asked, though I was pretty sure I knew the answer already. He *was* angry at me. At the situation. At everything, if his demeanor was anything to go.

He turned onto the road and started driving out of town. "No. Why would I be?"

I lifted my hand and swirled my hand in his direction. "I'm getting a whole lot of angry vibes over here, for one thing. And you stormed out of the café without a word or explanation."

He sighed.

I waited for him to say something. I was more patient than Ruby and Tiffany, but damn it was hard to wait him out. I began to recite spells in my head, practicing, testing myself—to see how many I remembered by heart.

"I'm not angry at you," he finally said, breaking the silence. "Just, this whole *mess*."

"You mean your pack not having enough females for you to mate with?" I asked. That was something I really wanted to help the pack fix if I could. Without the ability to give birth to daughters, the pack's blood lines would soon be dead and gone. Once I'd sorted out my own situation, of course.

He sighed. "Partly. Hang on. What do you know about that?"

I swallowed hard and lifted my legs so that my feet were on the car seat, and I could hug my knees like a physical shield against my heart. "Just so you know," I began, "I have this... thing with being honest. I like to tell the truth as much as possible and prefer other people to be the same. Even if its uncomfortable or whatever."

I'd learnt that the hard way when I hadn't told Ruby about what I'd done with the spell last year. And now with my mom's lies about my dad. The truth was just better, no matter how hard it was to admit to.

Elliot nodded. "Fine by me. So, tell me what you know."

"Basically, twenty-three years ago, three cousins from your pack went missing, and ever since then, there's been no females born to your pack. Correct?"

Elliot nodded. "Pretty much."

"How old are you?" I asked. "Because there should have been heaps of females around your age born... or do I assume incorrectly?" He had to be older than me, by quite a bit if I wasn't mistaken.

"I'm almost thirty-five, so yeah, there were a lot of females for Tommy and me, in our years."

Thirty-five. Shit. He's so much older than me! I swallowed down the response that would point out just how young I was. My mom wasn't going to like this at all, despite her encouragement to chase love. "And you still didn't get married?"

Elliot shrugged. "I was waiting for my Fated mate. I wasn't going to just... mate some woman who wasn't meant to be mine."

His poetic and strangely possessive words fell around me like a spell and I shivered. Despite his huge, gruff, exterior, it was obvious this wolf shifter believed in the magic that drew two people together. Or in our case, four people.

He glanced at me as we drove closer to my house. "What's that got to do with the Manterri cousins?"

I sighed. "Long story short, one of those men was my father."

Elliot's arms flinched and he swerved.

"Whoa!" I yelled, grabbing hold of the 'oh shit' handle above the door, as Tiffany liked to call it.

He swerved back into the lane. "Are you telling me that you're half wolf shifter? That's why you're my mate?"

"Well, according to my mom, my dad was half warlock, but yeah, there's wolf shifter in me, too."

Elliot shook his head as if the puzzle pieces were finally falling together. "It's all making sense now."

I swallowed hard. "There's more."

"More what?"

"More you need to know."

Elliot gripped the steering wheel tighter, his knuckles showing white in the fading sunlight. "I'm game. Hit me with the truth, Bella."

If he hadn't been driving, it would have been laughable how intense this conversation had gotten. By the way my heart was pounding in my chest, my whole body knew how dangerous a situation I was in.

I drew my magic into my fingertips, ready to cast a spell to transport us both to safety if anything untoward happened. Like Elliot swerving the truck off the road entirely. My heart dropped, but I forced myself to say this next part in a rush. This piece of truth almost lost Ruby her mates, and I wasn't going to make the same mistake. "Last year, Ruby, Tiffany, and I cast a love spell that would bring our soul mates to us."

Elliot frowned. "Why would you do that?"

His reaction was unusually calm, so I relaxed a little. "Because all three of us grew up without fathers. Our mothers were, and still are, all single. Their hearts were broken. We didn't want that same fate for us. So, we all swore when we were teenagers to not date and wait for the right man to come along. Plus, the warlocks in our coven were always super suspicious of us and never wanted to date us anyway. In retrospect, it was probably the wolf shifter genes that put them off."

That was something I'd never really thought about before this minute but made sense now that I was hashing it out. Of course, none of the boys in town, human or warlock, wanted to date us. Our wolf shifter genes would have scared them all off!

"And when you say love spell, it doesn't make us fall in love with you, right?"

I shook my head. "Oh, no! It's nothing like that. It just encourages Fate to put our soul mates in our path, earlier. It can't make you feel anything that's not real."

Elliot slowed down the car as we drove down the main street of town. "You're going to need to give me directions on where to go."

I directed him left, then right, then over to where my mother's house was. "Just there. The house with all the flowers in the front yard."

My mom was a bit of a hippy. She wore bright colors, had long flowing hair, and liked flowers all around her. I for one loved how different she was.

Elliot pulled up and turned off the engine. He twisted around to stare at me from the driver's seat. "Okay, so, you're half wolf shifter, well, a quarter wolf shifter. Your father is one of the Manterri cousins who went missing twenty-three years ago, and that is somehow linked to the lack of women in our pack. And you cast a love spell that sped up our meeting. Anything else I need to know?"

I blinked at him. "How are you so calm about all of this?"

Ruby's guys had all but flipped over this very thing.

He shrugged. "I already knew most of it."

My mouth dropped open. "How?"

"Jackson and I are cousins."

I slapped my hand against my forehead. "Oh, my God. Why didn't you stop me then?"

"I wanted to hear your side of the story as well."

I nodded slowly. "Okay, well, that's good to know." *The strong and silent type. Never thought I'd get one of those.*

Elliot shifted in his seat. "Do you think the cousins' disappearance has much to do with our pack's population problem?"

I nodded. "I'm not meant to say anything yet, not until we investigate it more, but yeah, I do. It sounds like someone cursed your pack. Why? I don't know. How? Same. No idea." I bit my lip. I hated knowing so little.

Elliot stared out the windshield. "I suppose it doesn't really matter now, and it's not like you had anything to do with it. You weren't even born yet."

I dropped my feet to the floor and unbuckled my seat belt. "I can't believe you're being so calm." I opened the door to the truck and got out, a little in awe of the guy who'd driven me home. Ruby's guys had lost their shit over the fact that we'd used a love spell to find them. Was Elliot really that much cooler?

He got out of the car too, walked around the hood, and leaned against it.

I stared at him, drinking him in. He was hot. Too hot for me. Mature with a

huge body. Thick thighs. Massive shoulders. Then there was his face. *Damn it.* Those eyes were those of an angel and devil, mixed into one.

"Come here," he said, and held out his hand.

I glanced around. This was my neighborhood. What if someone saw and told on me? What if my mom saw me?

"Come here," Elliot repeated.

I walked forward and took his hand.

He pulled me into his body so that our hips were connected and he was staring down at me. "Have you kissed either of the guys yet?"

I nodded honestly. "I kissed Jonah yesterday."

Elliot grabbed me around the waist, spun us around, lifted me up, and put me on top of the hood of his car.

"Tommy?" I shook my head, swallowing hard against the nervous shivers coursing through me.

Elliot cupped my face with his huge, strong hands, his skin hot against mine. He tilted my face up to him.

I could hear the frantic hammering of my heart in my chest.

He was so much taller than me that even though I was sitting on the hood of the car, I still had to stretch up to meet his lips as he came toward me.

I wanted to get even closer. I slid my hand up his chest, connecting with hot, hard muscle.

Then he pressed his lips against mine so sweetly, hot tears gathered in my eyes.

I surged up to get closer, wanting a deeper contact.

He groaned in his throat and pressed open my lips with his, stroking his tongue through in search of mine.

I moaned in return, wrapping my arms around his neck to pull him closer.

His hands left my face and slid lower, grabbing a hold of my ass and dragging me hard against his body.

I gasped against his mouth, both terrified by the huge, hard lump between his thighs, and aghast at my body's reaction to it. My belly melted like a hot pool of lava, then began to tighten and throb with yearning. The desire for Elliot rose up so hard and so fast inside of me it felt like he was working a spell on me. My hands were everywhere, and I was moaning like a wanton in some porn film.

I was out of control. I didn't care if it was meant to be this way, or if, because he was my mate, this would be considered 'right'. It was too much, too fast. I wanted him too much. This couldn't be normal. I pushed my hands hard against his chest.

He lifted his head, staring down at me with eyes that had partly shifted.

"Please stop," I said, though my open thighs shook with the need to wrap themselves around his waist and pull him tighter to my body.

He growled softly in his throat, grimacing as he stepped back. "What happened? Did I do something wrong?"

I slid off the hood of his car and on trembling legs I walked over to my front door. "Nothing. You didn't do anything wrong." *Except remind me that I'm more of a woman that I realized.*

My front door opened, and my mother stepped out. She raised her hand as though to cast a spell.

Fear pulsed through me. I yelled out, "No!" and flung a protection spell around myself and Elliot, dragging him closer to me. I could hear his cursed complaints from behind me as he stumbled forward, ending up practically pressed against me.

"What the hell is that?" he asked.

My mom dropped her hand and stared at me; her eyes as round as the moon. "Who is this, Bella?"

I checked my mother's mood, and although she seemed stable, I wasn't ready to drop my shield just yet. Ruby had told us how the moms had magicked her boys back to the pack grounds when they'd seen her kiss Jackson. I didn't want Elliot to have any more reasons to distrust us witches. "This is Elliot. One of my soul mates."

Mom's eyes bugged out of her head. "So, it's true? You have three just like Ruby?"

I nodded. No point lying, not that I ever would to my mom. "Yes. I have three. Just like Ruby."

My mom's mouth opened and closed.

I felt her energy change, and I dropped the shield.

Elliot stumbled away.

I turned toward him.

His eyebrows were lowered and there was an angry glint in his eyes.

I didn't understand what he was angry about now. "What...?"

"Don't you ever do that to me again." Elliot growled, spun on his heel, then stormed off.

I stared after him.

He jumped in his truck and drove off without another word.

"But you don't even know what I did. Or why," I whispered, because I knew he'd never hear me, even if I yelled them.

Mom's arm came around my shoulders. "I don't think he liked being magically manhandled."

I glanced up at her. "What do you mean?"

She turned me toward the house and we started walking to the front door. "What you just did, wrapping him up in a protection spell and pulling him into you so I couldn't touch him? That's the magical equivalent of manhandling."

I sighed. "Seriously? I was trying to protect him!" *Stupid men.*

CHAPTER II
BELLA

I spent the night tossing and turning, worrying about Elliot. At one point, around one a.m., I'd been super close to just transporting myself into his house so that I could check on him and see if he still hated me for what I'd done.

But then I realized that if he'd had such a bad reaction to the small bit of magic I'd worked on him, he was unlikely to appreciate me teleporting right into his house. It was kind of breaking and entering, technically. *Sort of.* Plus, what if he slept naked? The idea filled me with so much desire, I was horrified. So, instead, I stayed in bed, writhing with unfulfilled lust and no small amount of embarrassment.

By the time I'd gotten up and helped Mom prepare for Thanksgiving lunch at Ruby's house, I was practically gasping with unsatiated need.

"What's up with you this morning?" Mom asked as we got in the car, ready to drive over to Ruby's new place. "You're like a cat on a hot tin roof."

I sighed and glanced out the window, watching the town fly by. "I'm fine. Just worried about Elliot." *And the fact that I have no control when I'm around him.* What was with that kiss? I'd been ready to let him take me, in whatever way he wanted. And that scared me. How was it possible to want someone on that level? Someone I barely knew.

I'd never really thought about the chemistry that existed between two people. Or the sexual attraction and connection that would build between me and my soul mate. And yet here I was, smack bang in the middle of everything I didn't want. Three men. Sexual attraction galore.

I groaned and crossed my arms over my chest, my nipples tingling uncomfortably. This was ridiculous. Maybe there was a spell I could do to counteract this? Or at least tone it down? I felt like I was going to explode with desperation!

"You're going to have to direct me," Mom said. "I don't know where I'm going."

I shook myself. "Oh, yes. Sorry, turn into the pack's town, and drive right up Main Street."

Mom did as I told her, driving slower than the speed limit.

"Mom, you can go a little faster."

"I know. I'm just looking around."

Or looking for someone, perhaps? I smiled at her as she practically stuck her head out the window to see everything.

"Did you look for him, Mom?"

She glanced over at me, then turned back to the road. "Of course,

I did. I even cast searching spells and did scrying for months—looking for him and the others. But nothing showed up. It was like they'd become ghosts and vanished from the face of the Earth."

Or cursed, I mused. "Turn left here." I directed Mom to Ruby's house, and we pulled up behind her mom's car.

"Looks like Sherie is here already," Mom said with a more relaxed tone.

I nodded, glancing around. Were my men here already? Would they come today?

"Let's go." Mom grinned and grabbed the food she'd made: a scrumptious pumpkin pie, a special, organic, hippy-style quinoa salad, and a seriously colorful fruit platter.

The latter was my request since my stomach was churning with anxiety and I didn't want to have to eat 'heavy' food all day. I grabbed the salad and the pie.

We headed across the road and up the garden path to Ruby's new home.

"Impressive," Mom said, glancing around at the quiet, clean neighborhood.

"The house is as well," I told her. "Haven't you been in the wolves' town before, Mom?"

She shook her head. "Not really. I think I came here and met your father once or twice, but it was so long ago. The memories fade with time."

I tilted my head at her. "It's strange to hear you talk about him so casually now." Unlike throughout my whole life, when my father was practically the only banned subject.

A pink hue flushed her cheeks. "Well, it's kind of nice that everything's out in the open, now."

Not yet it's not. Not until we know what happened to our fathers.

The front door opened, and Ruby burst out. "You're here! Come in!" She ushered us inside with a flurry of noise and commotion.

The lounge room was abuzz. There was rock music playing, and the table had been set for ten. I glanced around, noticing extra changes that I hadn't made. A silver gilded mirror, another rug, and a few more decorative throw pillows. Someone had clearly been busy. Was it Ruby? Or her mom, perhaps?

The painting I'd magically created was still the only hanging picture adorning the space. I walked over to stare at it, a smile full of pride lifting my lips.

"You did a great job with that," Billy said casually as he walked up next to me.

His voice sent a small shiver down my spine, and I rubbed my hand over one of my arms to warm the now-goose-bumped flesh.

"Thanks. I haven't seen you guys in wolf form yet, so I hope I got it mostly right." I glanced up at the picture. "I can change anything in it, really."

Billy shook his head. "No. It's perfect."

I turned toward him and found him staring at me. I lifted an eyebrow. "Yes?"

He didn't smile, but something lit up in his eyes that looked like amusement. "I hear we're soon to be related."

I groaned. I'd almost forgotten two of my mates were brothers. And that their brother was Ruby's mate.

"News travels fast."

He shrugged. "It's a small town."

"You're pretty close to your brothers, I assume?" I asked.

Despite Tommy and Jonah being quite different, I could imagine there was a certain, unbreakable closeness among people who grew up together in the same household, especially if they were related by blood.

I couldn't imagine having siblings myself, not now anyway. My best friends, my *cousins*, were the closest thing I'd ever had to sisters.

Billy nodded, glancing up at the painting again. "I could never work out why I was black, and my brothers were white wolves. Especially when both our parents shift into gray."

I shrugged. "Well, black and white make gray." It kind of made sense to me.

Billy turned to me with a look that told me I didn't get it. "Ruby's wolves are all black. Yours are all white. Including Elliot."

I stared at him. "You think our mates are, what... color coded or something?"

Billy laughed and the sound was a harsh barking, like he didn't laugh very often. "Yeah, something like that."

I looked up at the picture, then back at him again. "I wonder if Tiffany will have the same thing?"

Billy grinned. "The blonde?"

I nodded. That was how most people saw Tiffany, as 'the blonde' one of our trio. She was so much more though, strong in a way I wasn't.

He shrugged. "You've got white. Ruby's got black."

"What's left?" I asked.

He frowned. "The rest of the pack is mostly brown."

I tilted my head. "Didn't you say that both of your parents are gray?"

He nodded, though there were shadows in his eyes I didn't understand. "Yes. But the gray wolves are rare now."

I started to ask what he meant, but the front door opened, and I shivered. Not from the cold, but with awareness and premonition. *My men were here.* I turned to face the hallway that led to the front door. My breath caught in my throat, and I froze as all three sets of eyes zeroed in on me. I couldn't move.

The whole room seemed to be holding their breath in preparation for what would happen next.

Jonah stepped away from the two, hulking Alphas and moved over to me. "Hey, beautiful."

I managed to smile, though my knees were starting to give way. "Hey."

The room broke into a cacophony of noise as all the men greeted each other and Ruby was at the center of the hurricane.

My mom stood with Sherie in the kitchen, watching the maelstrom with a strange look of envy.

I frowned. Were they really jealous of us? What for? For finding these men? I stared, feeling for the vibe of our moms and yes, it came back the same. *Jealous.*

They must really miss their men, I thought, a twinge of sadness for them snaring inside of me.

"What happened last night?" Jonah asked, leaning close and whispering against my ear, all the while pressing a warm hand to the small of my back.

"What do you mean?" I asked. *Other than the hottest kiss of my life.*

He shrugged. "Tommy came back to the pack, mad as a cut snake. You two get into a fight, or something?"

I shook my head. "Not really, but I used some magic, and I don't think he liked it."

"Is that it?"

"Yep."

Jonah turned back to the group with a shake of his head. "Weird."

Ruby began to take control of the room, throwing her hands and voice about. "Lunch is served. Grab a plate. Help yourself. Sit wherever you want!"

The guys all grabbed plates, and single file, filled their plates with all the trimmings. Turkey and pork, pies and bread, salads and roast potatoes.

I stood back and watched, standing with the moms.

When the men were finally settled at the table, I got my plate, filled it with whatever I thought I could stomach, then slid into one of the only remaining chairs—in between Jonah and Ruby.

The conversation flowed well, and the food was beautiful. Ruby's mom magicked up more dessert when the first platters were empty; but I couldn't eat half of my main meal, let alone dessert. My stomach was in knots. What was I going to do about my men? I needed something to distract me.

I turned to Ruby who sat to my left. "I want to go speak to some of the Coven about the high warlock and try and find out what he might have done to our moms twenty-three years ago. You want to come along?"

Even though I'd spoken very quietly, the whole table of six wolf shifters stopped talking, and turned to look at me.

An embarrassed heat flushed up my cheeks and I stared at the wooden table, unable to take the pressure of all six men staring at me.

Ruby laughed. "Shifters have exceptional hearing. You'll never get away with whispering ever again."

I risked glancing up and was mortified to see them all staring at me still. My gaze shifted to my mom, who was sitting with Sherie and looking perplexed.

It was Darren, the part-warlock, who leaned forward and spoke to me first. "What do you mean, exactly? Ruby told us what your moms told you guys about the spell, and that you assume it's linked to the lack of females in our pack."

I looked over at Ruby.

She threw her hands up. "I don't keep secrets from them. Sorry."

I pressed my lips together, unsure how much to share.

Jonah's hand slid across my thigh and squeezed. "It's okay. Just tell us what you're thinking. Everyone here knows that you weren't even alive when it all went down."

"They're right," Sherie said, interjecting. "If anything, they should blame us for what happened."

I shook my head. "But we don't actually know what happened, and that's what I want to find out."

"Why?" Jackson asked, taking another slice of pumpkin pie and placing it on his plate. "I mean, there's nothing you can do now, is there?"

I tilted my head. "Well, it truly depends on what was done."

"What do you mean?" Darren asked, staring at me intently.

I took a deep breath, "Well, if my instincts are correct..."

"And they usually are," Ruby added with grin.

I continued as though she hadn't spoken. "Then the high

warlock at the time created a spell that got rid of our fathers and cursed the women of this town so that they couldn't have any more daughters."

The whole table was listening to me, and although I kept staring at the table to avoid their gazes, I had to push through the uncomfortable feeling so that I could keep talking and share the truth as I knew it.

"Yeah, but the high warlock's gone," Ruby said from her place beside me. "He died what... two years ago?"

I looked at Jonah. "And there's been no girls born in that time?"

He shook his head. "None."

I nodded, running through the components of the spell. *What would have been required to harness that much power?* I tapped my fingers on the wooden table. "Then the curse has to be linked to either our mothers or us. If we can sever that tie, then maybe there's a chance we could lift the curse."

No one spoke.

I risked a glance up. I met Tommy's gaze because he seemed the least intimidating of all these virtual strangers.

"So, does that mean you might be able to fix the pack's problem?" he asked hopefully. "Make it possible for our women to have daughters again?"

"You might be able to save the pack," Jackson said from the other side of the table, his eyes wide.

I nodded. "That, and more."

"What more?" Jackson asked.

I swallowed, finding it harder than usual to be honest in this moment, but they deserved the truth. "I want to find out what happened to my father."

CHAPTER 12

BELLA

Ruby reached over and squeezed my hand. "They're gone, Bella. They've been missing for twenty-three years. For all we know they might even be dead."

I twisted in my chair to stare at her, anger flaring brightly in my chest. "How can you say that? You might've met your dad when you were young, and he was a wolf. What if the high warlock cursed them to their wolf forms, forever? Unable to communicate or shift back to human. What would they do? Where would they go?"

Ruby stared at me, her eyes wide and a little hurt.

I sighed. She wasn't the one I should be asking. I turned

around to stare around at the table of wolf shifters. "Do you guys know? Would they hang around here? Would they go to another pack?"

Elliot and Tommy glanced at each other.

Then Tommy looked at me. "You need to speak to the pack elders."

"Why?" I asked. "Would they know?"

"Elliot and I heard them talking about the Manterri cousins, years ago, now. We were, I don't know, maybe fifteen at the time?"

Elliot pressed his lips into a thin line but didn't say anything.

They'd been fifteen, so assuming Tommy and Elliot were the same age, that was some twenty years ago.

"What did they say?" I pressed.

"That they'd run into a small pack of wolves that looked like the Manterri cousins. They were distinctive because they were the same size, same age, and all three of them were gray."

A sense of premonition shot down my spine like a bolt of lightning. *That was them!* "So, what happened after that?"

"They said that if the guys wanted to come back, they could. But they had to apologize to the whole pack first, for what they'd done."

My mouth dropped open. "What did they do?"

Tommy shrugged. "We don't know. They never told us. And we were kids, practically. We weren't part of the council."

I nodded, putting all the pieces together. "So, our fathers could very much be alive." I swallowed hard as emotion rose. What would my father look like? What would his voice sound like? And if the three men had been in wolf form for twenty-three years, would there be much of their humanity left?

"There's no way of knowing if they're still out there, Bella," my mom said softly. "I told you; we did so many location spells trying to find them, but we never could."

I ignored my mom. She'd been heartbroken and pregnant and had assumed my father had abandoned her twenty-three years ago. I didn't really believe her when she said she'd tried *everything* possible to find him. I looked at Tommy and Elliot, my Alphas. "Can you organize for me to speak with the elders?"

"Me too!" Ruby piped up.

I bit my lip. "We'll probably need to include Tiffany as well. She won't want to be left out of this, especially as her father was involved, too. Where is she, by the way?"

Ruby shrugged. "She said she had to work, but I think she didn't want to deal with us and all our mates. It'd be hard for her."

The words hung in the air, and I swallowed hard, trying not to blush. It was still so new, and such a surreal thing to acknowledge that I'd found my soul mates. *And Tiffany hadn't.*

"Yeah, you're right. She must be feeling left out." I tried not to look at my men, but my gaze swung with unerring accuracy toward Elliot and Tommy.

They stared back with an intensity that made my chest ache.

Tommy nodded. "We can arrange something."

I smiled at him, wanting to tell him how grateful I was for their help, but now wasn't the time to be super gushy. "Thank you."

With that sorted, Ruby soon moved the conversation into less fraught waters and the rest of the afternoon passed quickly.

I managed to follow along with the conversations, but inside my mind, I was consumed by questions. Mostly about my father, and where he'd been for the last twenty years. I couldn't even imagine having a father in my life now. Like I couldn't imagine having three soul mates. And yet, wanting Jonah, Tommy, and Elliot in my life was a lot more natural than I could have ever dreamed. *Perhaps having a father would be the same?*

When the kitchen was packed up and the festivities were over, Mom and I began to grab our bags.

Tommy and Jonah stepped forward and greeted my mom.

"We didn't officially meet," Jonah said, standing quietly by.

I smiled at my sweet Beta and turned to my mom. "Mom, this is Jonah and Tommy. They're Billy's brothers."

"Brothers? As in, you're both Bella's mates, and you're brothers?"

Her shock relating to my situation had officially reached a whole new level.

I turned to Mom and whispered, close to her ear, "They don't touch each other, Mom." Then I turned to where Ruby had moved to stand beside me. "Do they?"

Ruby laughed.

Jackson slung a possessive arm over her shoulder. "There's no crossing swords around here."

I frowned at Jackson. "Crossing...?" *Oh, my God.* I turned to my mom, heat warming my face. "Time to go."

"Actually," Tommy said, interjecting. "We were hoping you'd hang around a bit and we could have some time with you. Alone."

"Alone," I repeated, assuming I would never be *alone* again. "As in, the four of us?"

I could feel Ruby practically vibrating with excitement, but she was holding herself together.

"Bella, I'm not sure about that..." Mom began.

I turned to her and gave her a stern look. "I'll be fine." A virgin I may be. But a child I was not. And these were the men that both Fate, and my magic, had decided I should be with.

Tommy cleared his throat and glanced at the floor. "Ah, it'll be the three of us. Elliot had some work to do on a house. But we could catch up with him later."

My gaze shot around the room. "Where is he?"

"He already left."

Disappointment washed over me like a tidal wave. I wasn't sure why. Two days ago, I would have been terrified about the idea of handling three men at all, let alone, at once. Now, I felt so rejected. My throat tightened and I had to force myself to swallow the lump that rose. "But... why? He seriously had to work?" *On Thanksgiving?* I didn't believe it.

Tommy glanced away.

Jonah grinned. "What's wrong, beautiful? We're not enough for you?"

His tone was light-hearted and humorous, but something behind the words made me stop and assess what I was about to say next. Balancing all their needs was going to be a challenge, especially with the jealousy aspects of brothers and best friends. Not to mention the competitive nature of men to begin with.

"It's not that. I'm just worried about him." I said. "We had a bit of a fight, or something, last night. I know he's mad at me and I just wanted to sort it out."

Jonah's posture relaxed.

Tommy grinned at me. "Don't worry about Elliot. When he's got his back up about something it's better if you just let him be. He'll work through it."

I wanted to believe Tommy. After all, from what I'd gathered, they'd been best friends their whole lives. But something told me that more time apart was just going to tear us asunder. But how was I going to tell these two that? All I was going on was a gut instinct and premonition.

"Okay. I'll trust you know him better than me." I put my bag on my shoulder and kissed Ruby goodbye. "Thank you so much for lunch and it was great to catch up." I waved to Ruby's men, then kissed Sherie on the cheek. "See you all soon."

My mom walked me out, her nervous aura making me want to shake her.

"Stop it," I said when we were way down the path, elbowing her gently in the arm. "They're not going to hurt me."

"Just take this with you," Mom said, tugging off one of her bracelets and pressing it into my palm. "It's a locator and will bring you straight home if you need it."

I almost rolled my eyes at how protective she was being but tried to empathize. I tried to imagine what it would be like to be in her shoes, watching her only child walk away with two huge wolf shifters intent on seducing her. "Thanks, Mom. I appreciate that." I hugged her tightly. "I'll be home later, okay."

"Do you want me to come get you?" Mom asked, as she pulled

her car keys out of her bag, the keys jingling a little more than normal.

"We can drive Bella home later," Jonah offered.

"I'll call you if I need a lift, Mom, thanks."

Jonah took my hand and pulled me into him.

We both watched my mom stiffly walk to her car and hop in.

Tommy stepped up next to me. He chuckled as she drove away. "She's so worried about us," he said. "I thought she was about to magic you back to your house just so she could save you from us big, bad, wolves."

I laughed as I turned toward the big Alpha, the only one I hadn't kissed of my three mates. "Well, compared to most witches, my mom is very open-minded. It's probably how she ended up falling in love with a wolf shifter in the first place, even though it was forbidden."

"Forbidden? Are you serious?" Jonah asked.

"Yeah, I read about it years ago. Marrying outside of the Coven has always been forbidden. Some human marriages were allowed, but they had to be approved." And that was another reason Tiffany, Ruby, and I had assumed our fathers were warlocks. They were the only ones that our mothers should have been associating with.

"Well, I'm glad your mom fell in love with a shifter," Tommy said, grabbing me around the waist and pulling me from Jonah so that I was pressed against him, staring up into his bright blue eyes.

"And why's that?" I asked, though Tommy's intent was pretty obvious, and it wasn't to continue the conversation.

"Because they made you, and your wolf shifter genes made you our mate. It's perfect."

"Perfect, huh?" I slid my hands up his chest until I could feel the pounding of his heart beneath my palms. "Wouldn't you have preferred a wolf mate?" *Surely that would have been easier for them?*

Tommy grinned, his white teeth flashing as his hands kneaded the flesh of my hips, drawing me even closer. "Who am I to question Fate? It knows what I need more than I do." He dropped his head.

I lifted my chin, wanting to know what it would feel like to kiss him. To know that everything was just as right with him as it was with Jonah and Elliot.

Before I could finish the thought, Tommy kissed me.

A sweetness stole over me that I hadn't expected. It was soft, and gentle. I slid my hands up and gripped his head, dragging him closer. Deeper. Wanting more.

Tommy growled, deep in his throat and grabbed my ass, hard.

There it is. What I was looking for. It's not what I'd experienced with Elliot, *thank God.* This was controllable and not scary. Just a beautiful, smooth, soft roll of desire through my body. I opened my mouth and let Tommy explore me, reveling in the kiss and wanting more. Needing more. I wanted to know what was behind this desire, this lust, where our mating would finally lead us.

I pulled away from the kiss and stared up into Tommy's lust-drugged eyes. I felt so safe with this Alpha. There wasn't the wildness in him that I felt with Elliot. With Tommy there would be safety and control. "Where are you guys taking me so we can spend some time together?" I asked. Hopefully, it was somewhere more private than the street outside Ruby's house.

Tommy kissed me once more, lightly on the lips, then gripped my hand and pulled me down the street. "Our house is empty for the next few hours. Let's go check that out."

Jonah hurried to catch up with us.

I squealed as excitement hit me in the belly. But closely behind it, a wave of doubt settled in. What would Elliot say? How would he feel if I moved ahead to the next stage of our relationship with Jonah and Tommy? I shook off the thought and allowed Tommy to pull me into the unknown.

Elliot was the one who had chosen to leave us today. He was the one who had to live with the consequences of that choice. Not me—*I hoped.*

CHAPTER 13

TOMMY

Having Bella's hand in mine was like walking in paradise, a place I'd never known existed. Just touching her skin, and knowing she was mine, settled my wolf to a level I didn't know existed. My wolf was no longer scratching at me to run, to fight, to be on the constant move.

He was still there, inside my chest, but with my mate's hand in mine, as I pulled her toward our house so I could finally make love to her, my wolf was calm. We would finally have the mate we'd waited for all this time.

Jonah jogged ahead of me to open the door.

I swept our mate up into my arms and crossed the threshold.

She squeaked and grabbed my neck, pressing herself against me.

Our house was simple. It only had one living room with a spacious kitchen and dining area. We had two large bedrooms, each with its own ensuite. One downstairs next to the living area which was mine. And one upstairs, which was Elliot's.

Elliot and I had designed it with the impression we'd always live here together, growing into two grumpy old men. Single. Forever.

How things change. I walked straight into my bedroom, still holding my mate, and set her down on her feet.

She looked around, her eyes wide. "You're not giving me the tour then?"

I pointed toward the living room. "Kitchen. Bathrooms behind you."

Bella walked over to the bedside table and placed her mother's bracelet down. Then she turned around to look at the ensuite as though she wanted a tour of the house.

Screw that. I was desperate to hold her, touch her. "Come here, beautiful." I walked over to where she stood by the bed and grabbed her hand, pulling her into me.

She pressed a flat palm to my chest. "We're going slow, right?"

I nodded. "Absolutely."

Jonah had said something about Bella being a virgin yesterday, which didn't surprise me. She smelled of purity, and sweetness, in a way that only virgin women did, not that I'd sensed one for a very long time.

I cupped her face and kissed her.

Jonah moved around behind her.

I glanced up.

My brother was kissing her neck.

Bella moaned luxuriously.

And at that moment, I decided this whole teaming up thing could work out well. She'd get so much more out of both of us working on her. Despite how much it was going to kill me to go slow,

I wanted Bella to remember this, always. "Lie down on the bed, baby."

Bella lifted her head and stared at me. "I'm not sure..."

I smiled at her. "We won't go any further than you want. I promise." I led her to the bed and reached for her blouse. "Let me show you how good you can feel."

She turned her head to glance back at Jonah.

He walked up behind her and kissed her hungrily.

While she was moaning softly with her eyes shut, kissing my brother, I tugged her skirt down over her hips and lifted the hem of her blouse. "Arms up, beautiful."

She broke her kiss with Jonah and lifted her arms so I could tug off her top. Then she was standing in her underwear.

"Damn, you're beautiful."

Bella glanced down at her body and began to lift her arms to cover herself.

"Oh no," I said, swinging her up in my arms, then walking the few feet to the bed and placing her down on the soft mattress. "There'll be no covering up this perfect body."

I glanced at my brother. "You go up. I'll go down."

Jonah grinned at me and crawled onto the bed.

"What does that mean?" Bella asked, glancing up at Jonah.

Hovering over her, my younger brother smiled at our mate. "It means I'm going to pleasure the top of you, while Tommy takes care of you down below."

She sat bolt upright. "No! I... I don't think I can do this. It's too much."

I hadn't been expecting that reaction.

Jonah stared at me, his eyes wide and panicked.

I got up and slid onto the bed next to her, lying down on my side. "Come here, beautiful." I rolled her onto her side and stared at her beautiful face, cupping her cheek. "I want to make love to you. Will you let me?"

She swallowed hard. "I'm not sure I want to do... everything."

I nodded. "How about everything else but sex? I'll keep my pants on. And so will Jonah."

Her eyebrows rose. "So, I won't be able to touch you at all?"

I laughed. "I thought you wanted to keep some distance between us?" *Goodness, this girl was contrary.*

She bit her lip. "No. Can we just go slow. Please?"

I nodded. "Yes. And if you say stop, at any point, we'll stop. Promise. Okay?"

She nodded. "Okay."

"So, you trust us to do the right thing?" I asked, wanting her full consent though my plan was to pleasure her and leave myself frustrated. Tonight was just about Bella.

"Yes."

I lifted her chin and kissed her lightly on the lips. "Then let me love you."

She nodded.

I slid off the bed, going down onto my knees, and reached out to grab her thighs.

She cried out in surprise.

I smiled and grabbed her ass, hauling her close enough to eat. Then I glanced up at my brother.

Jonah was repositioning himself so that he could lay down and kiss her at the same time.

Satisfied with our team efforts, I looked down at my meal. "So beautiful," I said, as I ran my hand up her silky thighs and stared down at her soft belly. I dropped my head, pressing a kiss to her belly button and inhaled her scent.

She was wet and wanting me.

Or us?

I couldn't be sure, and I didn't think it mattered. The scent of arousal wafting up my nostrils was making my wolf go insane. I clenched my teeth. *She wants slow. Settle down.* I grabbed her ass and began to knead her supple flesh, glancing up when I heard Bella gasp.

Jonah was tweaking her nipples and sucking her flesh through her lacy white bra.

I pulled back and grabbed the waist band of her pale pink panties. "These need to come off, beautiful."

"The bra too," Jonah growled softly.

I moved to pull them down, but Bella called out.

"Hang on, let me do it." She inhaled sharply and frowned.

How?

And then her underwear was gone entirely.

I stared up at her. *Respect.* "That is a neat ass trick."

She covered her face with her hands.

I chuckled at her embarrassment. She was so strong and yet so sweet. So naïve and yet so instinctual. Our mate was a lot of things, and not all of them made sense, but she was perfectly our Bella. I stared down at her pussy lightly covered in soft, dark hair. Natural. *Nice.*

I pushed open her thighs and began to kiss the insides of her legs.

She resisted at first, but then Jonah began to work on her and she was soon distracted.

He suckled her nipples and kissed her neck and face, smothering her in intense, but tender passion.

Her legs relaxed as she did.

I moved closer to paradise. My own body throbbed, my cock hard in my jeans. I staunchly ignored the need to rip off my clothes and free my aching shaft. Bella needed to know that she could trust us, and I couldn't think of a better way to prove it to her than this. We would give her the most amazing amount of pleasure possible and take none for ourselves. She was our focus.

I kissed a path all the way up to her inner thigh, then moved up and licked across her belly and down, tasting her pussy for the first time. *Oh, fuck yeah.*

Bella gasped and grabbed my head, gripping my hair tightly.

Although I sensed she wanted to, she didn't pull me away. So, I waited, just breathing against her soft flesh.

She didn't move or try further to stop me.

Satisfied that she yearned to continue, I flattened my tongue and stroked it over her swollen clit.

She gasped again, the sound like music to my ears.

I moved lower, tasting her lips and her sweet juices.

Her belly contracted tight, and she half sat up, gasping even louder. She writhed in pleasure, arching her back and throwing her head from side to side.

I wanted—needed—to get closer to her. Carefully I slid up next to her, running my hand down her sexy little body, over her mons, and slid my fingers lightly over her wet folds.

She turned her head toward me, her lips parted on a gasp and her eyes widened.

Without a moment's hesitation I slid a long finger inside her.

She moaned, her eyes closing as she arched closer to me.

I pressed deeper, loving how wet and juicy she was. How her pussy gripped my finger tight. *Damn*, that was going to feel nice on my cock. I groaned as I thrust my finger in and out. "Bella, you feel so fucking good."

She turned her head toward me again.

I took the opportunity to kiss her, tasting her lips and groaning as she thrust her tongue forward desperately to meet mine.

"My turn," Jonah said, shuffling down her body so he could kneel between her thighs.

I didn't want to withdraw from her body, but I took my fingers out of her perfect pussy and wiped my hand on the sheets.

Jonah began to kiss her thighs.

"How you going, beautiful?" I asked her, cupping her sweet little breasts. They were perky, and pink-tipped, and fit my palm perfectly.

"I'm... ah!" She arched again. "I'm... I don't know."

Jonah began to work on her.

She thrashed her head as she experienced the pleasures that a man—*or men*—could give for the first time.

I smiled to myself. My balls were practically blue, I needed release so bad. But as a virgin who knew little of her body, I could only assume that Bella had no idea what she needed. She trusted us to guide her, to go slow with her. I got up on my elbows and leaned over her body, cupping her breasts and sucking on their delightful pink tips. Her nipples hardened in my mouth, and I used my teeth and my tongue to lavish them with love.

"Oh! Ah... Tommy, I... Can you—" Bella managed between shallow, gasping breaths.

Jonah came up next to her again, putting a hand on her belly in a possessive caress I didn't expect of the younger Beta. "What's wrong, Bella? Did I hurt you?"

"No," she said, shaking her head from side to side on the pillow adamantly. Then her gaze landed squarely on me. "Tommy, can you put your hand back... inside me?" She tugged on my arm, need written all over her beautiful expression as she led me back down between her thighs.

I grinned. "Need to come, baby?"

She nodded in agreement, though I wasn't sure she fully understood what I meant.

I slid my fingers over the swollen bud of her clit, circling the flesh.

She grabbed at me with urgent hands, her nails pinching my skin.

Then I slid two fingers inside her, feeling her gasp at being stretched.

She tightened around me like a perfectly fitted glove.

"Come on, beautiful. Come for us." I flexed my fingers inside of her with years of practice, hitting all the spots I hoped she'd love.

Her eyes began to roll back, and she reached for Jonah, turning her head and lifting her chin to kiss him. She gasped against his mouth.

I watched as she began to tense up, her pussy tightening around my fingers as I continued to gently thrust them in and out. I heard the front door open and shut but didn't think much of it. I couldn't pay it much heed, not when Bella was about to have her first orgasm in my arms.

She screamed out in ecstasy, and began to pulsate around my fingers, her belly shaking and trembling as she frantically rode her first ever wave of release.

I watched her face contort in rapture as she came down from its crest, then her eyes opened in wonder, and she looked up. Then she scrambled to sit up, her gaze one of shock.

I withdrew my fingers, worried I'd hurt her, and glanced toward the door.

There stood Elliot, taking up most of the door frame. With the light casting shadows around him, he looked like some sort of demon. He didn't so much as utter a single word, but as a growl rolled through his chest and his teeth flashed even in the dark, I *knew* we were all in trouble.

The hairs on the back of my neck stood up and I jumped to my feet, ripping off my shirt, putting myself between him and Bella.

If the Alpha wanted a fight, he was going to bloody well get one.

CHAPTER 14
ELLIOT

The sound of Bella's orgasm should have been the hottest, most amazing sound I'd ever heard in my life. But instead of getting to enjoy it, feeling it around me, and wanting to be a part of it—I stood practically a world away, in a doorway watching it happen. Cold and alone.

The rage of my wolf simmered deep in my gut. My mate was lying completely, gloriously naked, between Jonah and Tommy. Tommy had his fingers inside of her, juices glistening all over his hands. And Bella came for them, long and hard, her naked body writing on the bed as she screamed for them in the throes of passion.

The sound was like a knife in my heart. The betrayal ran deep, antagonizing old wounds. My hands clenched into tight fists, and a dark, possessive growl rolled through my chest. She was my mate. *Mine!* What the hell were they doing here without me in the first place?

My wolf rose up inside me and fast began to take over my human body. I had no hope of stopping it. Not now. It was dangerous. Closing my eyes, I tried to push him down, tried to stop him from emerging. There was no-one to fight here except the men I considered family and the woman who was my mate. But there was no pulling him back. It was an exercise in futility.

Tommy jumped from the bed, an expression of determination in his features.

Fur began to sprout from my skin and I dropped down to all fours, my clothes melting away as my wolf emerged, rearing for a fight. Then I launched at my oldest friend, teeth bared.

Bella

I WANTED to scream but my throat closed up and the sound was lost forever. I stared, horrified at the scene unfolding before me.

Elliot transformed into a savage-looking, snarling wolf.

Jonah threw himself in front of me.

Tommy got to his feet, the Alpha in him rising.

"What do we do?" I gasped out to Jonah.

"Your mom's bracelet," Jonah said, launching across the bed to where I'd put the piece of jewelry down on the bedside table. He thrust it into my hand. "Go. Quickly. We'll find you later."

Tommy had shifted already, and the two huge, growling wolves stood in the room, facing off against each other.

I didn't think, there was no time. I clutched the talisman, said the transportation spell in my mind, and closed my eyes. The sounds of aggression and feelings of terror faded away, and I was suddenly in a quiet room. I opened my eyes and looked around, instantly recognizing the location. I was stark naked on my mother's bed, and she was nowhere to be found. *Thank God.* I jumped to my feet and raced to the bedroom door, but it opened before I could get there.

"Bella!" Mom stared at me aghast.

Both of my hands went to my boobs, covering them up, and I awkwardly crossed my legs over in an attempt to protect my lower modesty. "Um..."

Mom flung her hand through the air.

I was suddenly wrapped in her dressing gown. I smiled in relief at the small mercy as I slipped my arms into the holes and tied the belt. "Couldn't remember where mine was?"

Mom gave me a half smile in return. "I panicked. You're lucky you didn't end up wrapped in a sheet. Or worse, my underwear."

I grimaced, pulling the dressing gown tightly around my body, my heart still thundering inside my ribs. "Thanks, Mom."

"What happened?" my mom asked. "Are you okay?"

I nodded, thankfully still in one piece. "Yeah, I'm okay." But my eyes were filling with hot tears, and it became apparent that I was probably not as okay as I thought.

Mom wrapped her arms around me and held me tight.

I buried my head into the corner of her neck and sobbed, releasing the pent-up tension and shock of what just happened with my mates. *What a day.*

"Did they hurt you, sweetheart?" Mom whispered. "Because if they did, the girls and I will make them pay, don't you worry."

The vehemence in her soft words made my tears dry faster than anything else could. I lifted my head, wiping away the wetness that still clung to my cheeks. "Oh no. You can't do that. They didn't do anything wrong. It wasn't them." It wasn't me either. It was just nature. Wolves and witches weren't meant to get along, let alone mate. We were too different.

"What happened, Bella?" Mom asked more softly, taking my hand and leading me to sit on the large blanket chest at the end of her bed.

I sat and picked up a purple throw blanket, pulling it over my lap for something to hold on to.

"Please tell me," Mom pressed, her lower lip wobbling as though she may start crying soon too. "I'm imagining the most horrible things."

"Oh, please don't," I said, before sighing. "Long story short. I went back to Tommy's house with Tommy and Jonah, and they decided to... try some stuff with me."

"What kind of stuff?" Mom asked, narrowing her eyes.

I rolled my eyes. "You know, Mom. Kiss me, and touch me, and... stuff!" *Damn.* This was embarrassing.

"So... good stuff, then?" Mom asked.

"Yes!" *Why was she assuming the worst?* "You were in love with a wolf shifter, yourself, Mom. And I'm sure he wasn't horrible to you. Why are you assuming that my men are... rough or something?"

Her face turned as rosy as Ruby's red hair. "Oh, well, you're right. Your father never did anything I didn't want him to."

That sounded slightly strange. Had he been rough, and my mother had liked it?

Ugh! Too much information! I shook the thought out of my head and concentrated on the conversation at hand. "Well, they didn't do anything bad to me either."

"So, why did you transport back here naked?" Mom asked.

I shook my head. There would be no hiding anything from my mom now. "Basically, I was with Jonah and Tommy, then Elliot came home unexpectedly and saw us."

"And he got upset?"

I nodded. "Yeah. Very. It was like—rage. He shifted into his wolf.

Then Tommy shifted into his. And Jonah told me to go. So, I did. It seemed like the best course of action."

Mom stared at me, then covered her mouth with her hand.

"What?" Was she horrified? Was she disgusted? "What is it, Mom? Tell me."

Then she began to laugh.

"Mom!"

"I'm sorry," she said through her laughter, a tear rolling down her cheek. "I just can't believe it. I've spent your whole life worried about you. Worried that you'd find out who your father was. Worried about who you were going to marry in future. And now? You have three huge, possessive, jealous wolves fighting over you... and it's just too much."

I pouted. "Well, according to the boys, Fate decided I was the best person for them."

"Of course, you are, sweetheart. The love spell has ensured that outcome certain as well. It's just, I never imagined it would be like this for you."

I sighed heavily. "Me neither. I wasn't even sure I'd have a husband, or children."

Mom cocked her head at me. "Why not?"

I shrugged. "I don't know. It was just a feeling." I *did* know, though. My mom was sad and alone. I didn't want that for myself. So, avoiding all sorts of romantic relationships and entanglements had seemed like the right way to avoid that.

"So why did you do the love spell in the first place, then?" she asked softly.

"Because Ruby and Tiffany wanted me to."

Mom groaned. It was a long, drawn-out sound. "You know what I've always said about those girls. Just because they're you're best friends..."

"And my *cousins*," I added.

"And your cousins," she amended, "doesn't mean you have to be like them, Bella. You're different. You're special."

"Well, it doesn't matter now. I did it, and now I have two Alphas fighting over me, and then there's Jonah, of course." A strange laugh bubbled up in my throat. "I can't believe it, really. I have two guys fighting over me. It's insane."

"Three," Mom corrected.

"No, not really. Jonah doesn't fight. He's a Beta. Things between Jonah and Tommy are fine. They're happy to share me. It's just Elliot. He's possessive to a whole other level."

"So, maybe you need to choose just to be with them," Mom said.

The thought made my stomach swoop, and I forced down the bile that rose in my throat. "I'm not sure I can choose between them, Mom." The idea made me physically sick. Especially the idea of walking away from Elliot entirely. My connection to him seemed unusually strong.

Fate had sent me three men. The love spell wanted me to love all of them. Now that I'd started to fall for them, all for different reasons, I wasn't sure I wanted to give any of them up.

"Jonah seems like the sort of guy you should be with," Mom said. "He seems nice, protective as well."

Of course, that's who she'd suggest for me. The guy next door type. Sweet. Non-threatening. Nice and safe, but capable of taking care of her only daughter. "Was that what Dad was like?" I asked.

Mom's gaze zoomed back to mine, and I saw her carefully considering her words.

I raised an impatient eyebrow. "Well?"

Mom opened her mouth, then cleared her throat with a rough cough. "Um, no. Not at all."

"What was he like then?" I prompted.

Mom stared at her hands which were clasped in her lap. "He was strong. A lot more like Ruby's Billy, I'd say."

The bad boy. Damn, Mom. "I wish I could have met him," I said, and it was true. It always would be.

Mom reached over and clasped my hand. "Me too, sweetheart."

I stared at my mom for a long moment and felt her love squeeze me, wrapping me in a warm cocoon. Then I broke the look and stood up. "I better get dressed. Jonah said they'd come for me later—when they've resolved their wolfy issues, I guess." I began to walk toward the door.

"Bella?" Mom called out. "Think about what I said, yeah? Just because you feel attracted to all three men, doesn't necessarily mean you can be a family in the end."

I twisted around and stared at her. "But Ruby…"

Mom shook her head. "I told you, sweetheart. You're not like your friends. Perhaps three men is simply… too much. Just because Fate has offered you that many men, doesn't mean that you're meant to be with all of them. Maybe it's more about making the right choice for you?"

I straightened, feeling my stubborn streak flare. *No, that's not true. Fate sent me three men because I'm meant to be with all three!*

My mom put out a hand, obviously seeing the obstinance in my face. "Please, just *think* about it at least."

I nodded, conceding that it was something to consider. "I will." I left Mom's room and headed straight for the shower. I needed a moment to think and to wash away the scent of arousal that lingered on my body. Closing the door, I turned on the water, and shrugged out of the dressing gown. My nipples were tender, and my thighs were still slick with my own juices. *Ew.*

I stepped beneath the water and let the heat wash away Tommy's and Jonah's touch. If I had to, could I really choose between my mates? And who would I choose if I could?

Jonah was beautiful and young, like me. Happy and sweet. He'd be a good best friend for the rest of my life. I could trust him and rely on him. And kissing him was just heavenly. Surely, sex with him would be good, too?

Tommy was hot and dominant, which a secret part of me loved. He made me feel cherished. He'd look after me and perhaps encourage me to explore things and push myself in a way that Jonah and I just… wouldn't.

And Elliot, well, he made me want to strip off and mount him practically in the street. It actually frightened me how much I wanted Elliot. I didn't feel like myself when I was with him.

With Tommy and Jonah, I could be *me*—Bella the witch— without worrying about losing control. But with Elliot, a part of me was scared. I wasn't sure if it was the Alpha in him calling out to the wolf shifter in me, or if there was another reason for it. But our connection was... otherworldly.

Perhaps we'd been partners in a past life? Because a part of me recognized him; wanted to go down on my knees and serve him. And that went against everything else inside my rational mind.

I scrubbed my body and washed my hair, then finally got out of the shower and towel-dried myself. If I had to choose, Jonah was the safest bet. Jonah and Tommy, if I could choose two. We'd work well and easily as a little family. The guys, after all, were already family. Rationally, I would never choose Elliot as my one and only. He was all the things I wasn't. Passionate. Intense. And completely uncontrollable.

And then it hit me. *Elliot was my punishment for the love spell I'd cast.* Salty, hot tears stung my eyes. He was the curse and the gift all at once. To want someone so much who just didn't suit me, or the other men in my love triangle. My family. I sobbed softly as I brushed out my hair and wrapped a towel around my body so I could get dressed.

I hadn't been sure what my punishment would be for casting the love spell that took payment for its success, but the answer seemed to be staring me in the face. I couldn't have Elliot, no matter how much I wanted him. He would forever be the fire to my ice, and that would be my cross to bear. Even if it broke my heart to do so.

CHAPTER 15
TOMMY

I put an ice pack on my swollen eye and took a sip of the bourbon and Coke my brother had placed in front of me. Nothing like a drink to settle the stomach and take the edge off the pain of a fight—especially a losing fight.

"You need anything else?" Jonah asked me.

I shook my head and relaxed on the couch. "No, thanks."

Jonah collapsed onto the other side of the couch. "Where's Elliot gone? Do you know?"

I shook my head. "Nope. And at the moment, little brother, I don't give a shit." I would in the morning, though. Elliot and I had blown up at each other about shit in the past, but we always worked things out. It was one of the reasons we'd stayed friends all these years. We always put past grievances behind us, where they belonged.

"Do you think he'll forgive us for taking Bella to bed without him?"

I glared at Jonah, his question surprised me. "What do you mean, will he forgive us? There's nothing to forgive. We didn't do anything wrong."

"Didn't we?" Jonah asked, giving me a steady stare.

I took a long drink of my bourbon then rolled my eyes at my baby brother. "Listen, Junior. Stop getting all smart with me, okay? Elliot wouldn't have thought twice about us if he'd gotten to Bella, himself. He's just sore he wasn't the first."

And that was all it was. The stupid idiot was jealous as fuck, and being possessive over something that shouldn't have those sorts of rules. Loving our mate shouldn't be a competition about who could give her the most or the best. She wasn't a pie to divide and hoard in individual pieces.

"We've got our whole fucking lives to be with Bella. Why did he have to go all wolf and freak her out?" I said.

Jonah held up both hands. "Don't ask me."

I sobered, then took another drink. "That was good thinking, by the way. Getting her to, you know, magic out of here."

Jonah grinned at me. "Did you hear that bit?"

I nodded. "We're a good team. I was too focused on the threat to think about getting Bella to safety. So, nice job."

For a kid of barely twenty-three, Jonah had some guts about him. It made me proud.

Jonah shrugged. "As you said, we're a good team. It's probably why these witches need three of us. You know, to cover all the bases."

"Yeah. I suppose." I hadn't thought of it like that until now. "What do you mean, exactly, though?" I'd had a few bourbons now, and the pain in my head from the fight with Elliot was hammering away at what little thinking ability I had.

Jonah shrugged again and ran his hand over a nearby pillow. "Well, you know, we can be different things for them. Like, with Ruby, she's got a dominant Alpha, a tough Beta, and a part warlock who doesn't listen to anyone. With us, I'm the Beta, you're the Alpha. She gets fun, lighthearted me, and protective, strong you."

I frowned. "And Elliot?"

Jonah pressed his lips into a thin line. "I'm not sure where he fits, honestly."

I sighed, taking another swig. "Yeah, me neither."

Elliot had always been like a super-Alpha to me, and to most of the pack. No-one could beat him in a fight. He was angry almost all the time and had been since we were kids.

"Look, he'll come home later, and we'll sort all this out. Like you said, if Bella needs all of our different strength, we have to figure this out—or her."

Jonah glanced at his phone. "All right, well, I told Bella I'd find her later, just to check up on her. I don't have her number, though, so I might drive into town. You want to come?"

I shook my head. "It's probably best she doesn't see me like this." I indicated my bruised face. "Do you know where she lives?"

Jonah frowned. "No. Maybe I'll go ask Ruby."

"Get her cell number too, while you're there, let her know you're coming."

Jonah stood up and walked toward the door. "Will do. Be back in a bit."

I put my head back and closed my eyes. I needed a rest before Elliot got back. He'd already kicked my ass once tonight. I didn't want to hand him another victory on a silver platter.

~

Jonah

"Thanks for your help, Ruby," I said to the young, flame-haired witch, and headed to my car. "Appreciate it!"

"I'll text her and tell her that you're on the way," Ruby called back.

"Great!" I got in my car and headed into town, excited to see my mate again. After so many of my brother's generation had ended up single, I'd never assumed I'd be lucky enough to end up with a mate. Especially one as beautiful, smart, and talented as Bella.

I found her house easily enough thanks to Ruby's instructions and pulled up outside the quaint little two story.

Bella jogged out to greet me with a big smile on her face.

I jumped out of the car and grabbed her, wanting her lips on mine. "Hey."

I kissed her and she lifted her mouth to mine in greeting. A shot of triumph pulsed through me. *She wanted me.* Even as a Beta, and therefore the weakest of her three mates, she still wanted me.

She smiled up at me as she pulled back. "Thanks for coming to check up on me. It means a lot."

I grinned. "Of course."

"Do you want to come inside for a bit?"

I glanced toward the house. "Is it safe?"

She giggled, the sound gorgeous, light, and happy. "Yeah, of course. It's just my mom."

A full-blown adult witch. Yeah, nothing to worry about there. I let Bella tug me inside the small house and was overcome by how cozy it was. And colorful. There was patterned wallpaper and different types of carpet everywhere.

"Mom. Jonah's popped by to say hi," Bella called up the stairs.

"Hi Jonah!" her mother called down the stairs.

I smiled, though I couldn't see her. "Um, hi!"

"Kathy," Bella said.

"Hi Kathy!" Her mother didn't respond further, so I assumed I was allowed to stay.

"Come sit," Bella said. She wore a flowing pair of purple pants and a black tank that accentuated her tiny waist.

Lust hit me in the gut. Even with her hair half wet and hanging over her shoulder, she was still the most beautiful woman I'd ever seen. I sat on the brown couch littered with a dozen red cushions of varying hues.

"Come sit with me." I grabbed Bella's hand and tugged her down. She half landed on me, then leaned closer.

I kissed the top of her head and inhaled deeply. "Your hair smells good."

"Thanks," she said. "My mom makes our shampoo."

"Really? That's cool." I pulled her closer, fitting her into my lap so we were eye to eye. "So?" I asked. "Are you okay?"

"I am," she said, nodding. "What happened with Elliot and Tommy?"

I shrugged. "You know, Alpha shit."

"Who won?"

I raised my eyebrows at her. "Who do you think?"

Her smile faded. "Elliot."

I nodded. "He's the strongest Alpha of our pack. No-one has ever beaten him in a one-on-one fight." Nor a two-on-one, or even a three-on-one with the Betas.

Bella bit her lip in the sweetest, most worried way. "What does that mean? Is Tommy okay?"

"Yeah, of course he is. A bit beaten up, but wolves heal fast. We have super metabolisms."

She grinned. "I noticed; you guys don't have an ounce of fat between you."

I laughed. "We'll still keep you warm in winter, don't you worry."

She nodded, but glanced down, avoiding my gaze.

"Hey," I said, reaching out to take her chin in my hand and lift her face until she was looking at me again. "What's wrong?"

Her dark eyes brimmed with unshed tears, but she blinked them away. "Mom thinks I'll need to choose between you guys. She doesn't think I can handle all three of you. She thinks that just because Fate presented me with three men, that it doesn't necessarily mean I'm meant to be with all of you."

I laughed. How could I not? "What does your mom know about that? Has she tried having three men and failed, or something?"

She giggled, the tears disappearing. "Hardly. She dated my dad, got pregnant with me, and hasn't dated anyone since."

I brushed her hair behind her ear, loving being able to touch her so freely. "Then I'd say she isn't an expert on the subject."

Bella nodded, but the sigh told me there was more to it.

"Hey, come on, what's really up?"

She looked down and away, then finally lifted her face to look at me again. "I don't think Elliot and I are meant to be together."

My mouth dropped open. "Um, okay." *I doubt that very much from what I've seen.* "Well, that's easy then. Just you and me and Tommy. That'll be... easy." If that's what she wanted. Easy.

She nodded, her lips tilting up into a smile. "It would be, wouldn't it? So easy. And calm. I think that would work best."

My gut started to burn like I'd swallowed acid. I didn't like discussing getting rid of one of her mates so casually. I'd been mostly joking when I said we could get rid of Elliot. We couldn't, and I didn't think she really wanted to. She was just scared. Even talking about the subject felt like we were betraying Elliot, and I didn't like that feeling.

The guy and I had never been close. Twelve years my senior, we hadn't ever 'hung out'. But he was a respected member of our pack, and my oldest brother's best friend. He was loyal, and fierce, it was as obvious as the day was long, that Bella was his mate.

I swallowed hard. "You know that if you reject him, he'll never have another mate? That's not how this works."

Her eyebrows flew up. "What do you mean?"

She really hadn't thought this through properly.

I sighed, not sure how to tackle this, but determined to give her all the information so she could make the right choice. "I mean, if you don't want Elliot, or believe he's not your soul mate, then that's fine by me. But Elliot's wolf has chosen you, or Fate has chosen you as his Fated mate. Wolf shifters only have one. If you reject him, then he'll always be single. Not that you should worry about that—it's not your fault if the two of you don't click. I just want you to know that it's not like he can just go choose someone else if you don't him."

I shut my mouth, feeling like I was repeating myself and sounding stupid. Bella was saying she wanted to reduce her mates by one. That would give me more, not having to share her so much. I should be encouraging her, not trying to talk her out of it. *Then why does it feel so wrong?*

She slid from my lap and started pacing around the tiny lounge room. "It's not that I don't want him, Jonah. It's just that I don't think I can handle him! Look at how he responded to seeing me with you guys. He wolfed out, and Tommy got hurt when they fought. I can't spend my life like that, and neither can you guys."

I grinned at her. "Wolfed out. I like that."

She groaned. "It's true. And look at me," she said, throwing her hands around. "I'm not equipped to handle someone like that."

I wasn't sure exactly what she meant but agreeing with her seemed like the most appropriate course of action. I stood up and walked over to her. "It's all right. Whatever you decide you need, we'll find a way to make it work. Okay?"

She took a deep breath, then finally nodded. "Okay."

I didn't know if it was going to be that easy—actually, I was certain that breaking that sort of Fated bond was impossible—but at the rate Elliot was going, he was driving a big enough wedge between him and Bella, he may never be able to remove it.

I reached out to her and grabbed her around the tiny waist. "I'm sorry, baby, but I've got to go, now."

I'd come to check on her, just as I said I would. Now, I wanted to get back home and check on my brother. Make sure Elliot hadn't come back and started another fight. Tommy wasn't up for another round. He'd been lucky to get away with only the few injuries he'd sustained as it was.

Bella stepped closer and lifted her chin to present her face to me.

I dropped my head and took her mouth in a kiss that had me hardening in my jeans.

She squirmed against me invitingly.

When I broke off, we were both breathing heavily. "I think you need to come visit us again sometime soon."

She nodded, her lips swollen and red. "As long as Elliot is all sorted out, I'd love to." She walked me to the door.

I took out my cell. "I'm going to get Tommy to contact some of the elders, by the way. Have you got college tomorrow?"

She shook her head. "No. It's a holiday after Thanksgiving. We go back Monday."

"Great. We'll organize something so you can talk to them about the Manterri cousins."

"Thank you, Jonah. I appreciate that."

I walked through the door and grabbed my keys out of my pocket. "No problem. If I was you, I'd want to know what happened to my parents, too."

She stood on the doorstep and grinned at me. "Do I get to meet your parents soon?"

I nodded. "If you want."

She smiled. "Do you think they'll wonder why all three of their sons have witch mates?"

I laughed. "Nah. They'll just be glad to get some grandchildren, I think. After all the issues the pack's had, and the worries about the next generation, they'll be fine."

Her mouth dropped open. "Kids. I hadn't even thought about that yet."

I stared at her, worry knitting my gut. "You want kids, yeah?"

She nodded. "I suppose so. One day." She bit her lip. "But I'm still in college. It'll be years until I'm ready for something like that."

I held up my hands. "Hey, I'm only twenty-three. There's no rush on my account."

"But Tommy…"

She didn't say Elliot's name, but I knew she was thinking about him, too. My brother and his best friend were already thirty-five. They'd like kids now, I was sure. But that wasn't up to them. Bella's body was her own and they'd have to accept that one way or another.

I shrugged as I strolled over to my car. "They're lucky they've got you at all, Bella. Let them wait." I waved at her before I climbed into the car. "Call you in the morning."

She waved in return. "Okay, see you tomorrow."

I pulled the door shut and drove off, intent on getting to Tommy and sorting out this Manterri cousin puzzle, once and for all.

CHAPTER 16
TOMMY

I set off for home, rubbing my shoulder as I walked. It still ached from where it had been snapped earlier by my supposed best friend. "Thanks, Elliot." *Jealous bastard.*

The elders had agreed to speak to Ruby and Bella, though I sensed some hesitation in the ranks. If it wasn't for the fact that Jackson had already made a stand about Ruby being his Fated mate, the whole 'witch mate' topic would still be too taboo to even speak about; let alone the possibility of having them accepted and living with the pack.

When I returned to our house, Elliot still wasn't home, and Bella had arrived.

She stood by her little beetle car and chatted happily with Jonah. When she turned and saw me, her whole face lit up and she smiled at me as though she hadn't seen me in forever.

My heart thumped hard in my chest, and I inhaled sharply against the wave of longing that passed through me. That was my mate. The woman meant for me and literally chosen by Fate. "Hey, beautiful," I said through the thick emotion clogging my throat. I grabbed her, pulled her close, and without hesitation planted a kiss on her soft, full lips.

She kissed me quickly, then pulled back. "Is Elliot here...?"

I shook my head. "The big idiot still hasn't come home yet." I growled to pretend I was outraged, but I was actually beginning to get a little worried.

He'd never *not* come back to the pack before, even when he was younger and had less control over his wolf. *Unless he'd made the mistake of climbing into one of the available beds in town?* None of the single female shifters would reject him if he'd wanted to be there. Hopefully he wasn't that dumb, though. Jealous and angry as he was, the last thing we needed was for Bella to see Elliot stumbling out of another woman's bed. Getting her to forgive him after something like that wouldn't be an easy task. Getting her to forgive him for yesterday's outburst was going to be hard enough.

"Great," Bella said, obviously a little more relaxed knowing Mr. Grumpy hadn't come back yet. "So, what's the plan?"

"The elders have agreed to chat with you and Ruby. Have you called... what's the blonde one's name again?" I kept forgetting.

"Tiffany."

"Right. Did you want to call her too? The elders want you guys there in the next half hour or so, so we better go tell Ruby."

"Let me check." Bella pulled out her cell and started tapping away. She waited a moment, then an immediate message came. "Tiff's caught up with doing something with her mom. I'll just tell her that we'll let her know what the council says, later." Bella typed back a message, then slid the cell into her bag again. "Shall we get Ruby?"

I nodded and took her hand, loving the feel of her fingers interlaced with mine. "Let's go."

We walked the few blocks over to Jackson's house, collected Ruby and Darren, then set off to the elders.

Hopefully the girls would find some of the answers they sought, because I got the feeling this mystery was a lot more complicated than any of us expected.

❧

Bella

NERVES TIGHTENED MY STOMACH, giving me the jitters. "What do you think they're going to say?" I asked Ruby as we walked along the street, grabbing her arm and linking my hand around her elbow.

Ruby pulled me closer. "I have no idea to be honest. Don't you think that if they knew where the cousins had gone, they would have tried to get them back by now?"

"I don't know." I grimaced. I really didn't understand any of this —but I wanted to. What was the likelihood pf our fathers still being alive? *Not a lot, probably.* But hopefully we were about to find out the truth, no matter how sad or ugly it might be.

The five of us—Ruby, Darren, Tommy, Jonah, and myself—made our way to a large house that looked like a rustic church. It had gorgeous stained-glass windows and a large, steepled roof.

"What is this place?" I asked, staring up at the impressive façade.

"It's the Council building," Jonah said. "It's where we hold mating ceremonies, and birthdays, and the council members have their meetings here."

"Oh. Cool." Sounded simple. Except for the fact that I was about to walk into a room with some of the most powerful and knowledgeable wolf shifters in the whole town. *Where's Elliot when you need him? I'd feel safer if he was here.* I took a deep breath and, with my stomach flip-flopping nervously, I gripped Ruby's arm as we made our way up the steps and into the council hall.

Darren opened the large door for us, and we stepped inside.

I gasped at the sparseness inside the hall. It was a little intimidating.

Three men sat on chairs upon a raised stage at the end of the room, but otherwise the space was empty.

"Come forth," one of the men said, his deep voice booming through the room.

I glanced at Jonah and Tommy, fear skittering down my spine.

Tommy smiled at me. "It's okay. Let's go."

Ruby and I shuffled up to the stage, trembling beneath the icy stares of the three older men. They looked well into their sixties, with graying hair, and wrinkled faces. But they still seemed strong, and confident beyond measure.

"Tommy. Introduce your mate," one of the men called, addressing the only Alpha in the room.

I narrowed my eyes at them. I didn't like that. What happened to them being a modern pack that didn't follow the traditional hierarchy? Jonah or Darren were perfectly capable of introducing us all.

Tommy took a step forward. "Elder Mason, this is Bella, mine and Jonah's mate. And I believe you already know Ruby."

The elder cleared his throat. "Yes, hello Ruby."

Ruby grinned up at them. "Hi." She didn't seem perturbed by them at all.

I lifted my chin and forced myself to be as fearless as possible.

"How can we help you today?" the loud one in the middle of the trio asked.

Ruby straightened up and spoke for us. "Our mothers told us the other night that our fathers were the Manterri cousins."

There was a shocked stillness in the air, and no-one spoke.

I stared closer and sent out a wave of premonition magic.

They weren't shocked by the news. *They already knew who our sires were.* They were simply shocked we'd finally found out—that the wolf was out of the bag, so to speak.

"You already knew," I whispered.

The man in the middle frowned at me. "Yes. We knew that three witches had fallen pregnant by wolf shifters belonging to our pack. The high warlock made sure we knew about that."

The men glanced at each other in anger.

I stared at Ruby, before turning my attention back to the elders. "He came here? Why?"

"To punish us," the elder said. "The warlock swore it was sacrilege, a mixing of blood lines that shouldn't exist."

My mouth fell open. We'd been taught as children that wolf shifters weren't to be trusted; that they were dangerous and baser animals. But this was a whole new level of discrimination and hatred. "What did you tell him?"

The elder shrugged. "That we welcomed anyone who was a Fated mate of our pack. If that was three witches, then we would bring them into our fold as equals."

I frowned. "That doesn't sound right." I glanced at Ruby who'd told me that Jackson and Billy had been horrified to find out their mate was a witch. They'd obviously been taught the same thing we had as children, that it was better to marry our own sort, or a human at the very least.

"Are you calling me a liar?" the elder asked.

His growly tone sent a shiver down my spine and I stepped back and away from his hatred.

Tommy came up behind me, putting his hands on my arms to steady me. "Bella was simply asking a question, elder," Tommy growled back. "We've told her that growing up, marrying outside of the pack was not encouraged. Especially not to the witches."

I glanced at Ruby again.

She nodded. "Jackson and Billy said the same thing."

The elders were lying. I stared back at the trio of older wolf shifters. I was tempted to send out a truth spell, but that was against our laws. Not that the wolves would know that, but for the moment I would wait and see if they could stomach telling the truth on their own.

There was silence as the three elders looked amongst themselves, then they turned to us and the man to the left said, "Well, it wasn't encouraged, but there are no laws against it. Darren's grandmother was a witch. Jackson's grandmother, a human."

"Then why—" I didn't even finish getting the question out.

The elder stood up roughly from his chair. "Because that damn warlock cursed us. He said that our pack's punishment would be to have our blood lines die out. That the last three females to ever be born of our blood lines would be witches."

I gasped at his ferocity as much as at the new information too. "We're the last of all females born to your blood lines? What about all the men who mated outside of the pack?"

The elders shook their heads. "None of the men who've mated outside our pack have been successful in breeding."

"What?" I demanded. "So, hang on. Those who were lucky enough to find their mate in this pack, from the girls born before us, they all had kids?"

One of the elders nodded. "Yes, but all have been sons."

"And all those who mated outside of the pack, to what... other wolf-born females...?"

"Have not had a single live birth between them."

My stomach dropped. "My God."

Ruby grabbed me and turned me to face her. "This is even worse than we thought, Bella."

"I know." We'd known that no other females had been born since we were, thus cutting off the mating ability of most of the pack. But we'd also assumed that those same unmated males could have just bred with women born of another pack, or even other humans.

"What are you talking about?" an elder called out to us,

But I was focusing on Ruby.

Her eyes were wide as she stared at me. "No girls. No children,"

I nodded. "Only males born to those of this pack, and if they breed outside the pack, then no children at all."

Ruby nodded. "This is more than punishment."

"This is revenge," I whispered. "It means that this pack will end up with dozens of lonely males, childless and miserable."

"Talk about torture. They have to watch their pack end with them." I shook my head. "The high warlock must have really hated them."

"What are you talking about!" an elder yelled at us.

I twisted around to glare at him. "You don't need to raise your voice at us! We're just trying to figure things out."

The elder blinked at me, as though stunned I'd answered back. "Well, we've been trying to work this out for twenty years."

I shook my head. "It doesn't make sense. Why would the high warlock hate the wolf shifters enough to curse you in this way?"

"We don't know," the elder in the middle said.

Despite his ambiguous answer, I felt another layer of truth beneath what he was saying. But I held back from pushing for more information because I was afraid of getting distracted from the real reason we'd come here today. I took a deep breath and squared my shoulders. "Do you know what happened to our fathers?"

There was another moment of still silence.

The elder to the left shook his head. "No."

I narrowed my gaze at them. "I don't believe you." I raised my hand and felt the fire of frustration burning within my heart. "Tell me the truth."

"Or what?" the elder in the middle said, standing up and staring down at me.

The wallflower inside me ached to shrink back from his gaze, but a new side of me had awoken since meeting my men. A new, stronger Bella. One that wanted the truth, at all costs. "Or I'll *make* you."

CHAPTER 17

BELLA

Jonah grabbed my arm, a note of panic in his voice. "What are you doing?"

I didn't flinch, nor drop my hand. "Jonah, take your hand off me, please. I don't want to hurt you."

The elders laughed.

"Hurt him? You're not that strong, little witch," said Mason.

Ruby giggled from beside me. "You underestimate Bella, Mason. She's three quarters magical and the strongest witch of any of us."

He growled at me, his eyes flashing silver. "Don't threaten me. You're no better than the warlock who cursed us."

I dropped my hand, the tingle of magic I'd conjured still pulsing through my fingers. I turned and twisted the magical spark into something new, filtering a gentle truth serum through the room. It would only last ten minutes or so, but hopefully it would be enough to get us the information we so desperately needed. With a sigh I let my shoulders slump, feigning defeat. "*Please*, just tell us—is it true that our fathers could still be alive?"

The elders stared at one another, shock infiltrating through them.

Then the third man, the one who hadn't spoken yet, turned to me. "You're my son's mate, are you not?"

I stared at him.

He rose from his seat. Easily the largest of the three by far. He was broader, taller, and there was something familiar about his mouth...

"You're Elliot's dad," I said finally.

He nodded. "My son doesn't speak to me."

"Why?" I asked, hoping the truth serum was beginning to work.

"His mother and I embarrassed him when he was younger. He hasn't forgiven me for leaving her." The huge man swallowed awkwardly.

I ducked my head, some of Elliot's angry intensity making sense now. "It's nice to meet you. Can you tell me if my father might still be alive?"

Mason hit Elliot's dad on the shoulder. "Tony. Don't."

My magic seemed to be working better on Elliot's father than anyone. He jumped off the stage and walked toward us. He was as big as Elliot.

I had to crane my neck to look up and into his intense blue eyes. "Is he alive?" I repeated, curling my wrist and lending more strength to the magic of the truth spell. "Please tell us."

Tony nodded. "We think so, but we don't *know* for certain."

"What do you mean? What happened to him?"

"We believe they shifted into their wolves and then couldn't shift back. There have been sightings of them over the years..."

"Did they come back to the pack?" I asked. "Did they come here looking for help?"

"Ask Mason." Tony indicated one of the other elders on the stage. "He knows."

I walked around Elliot's dad with a quiet smile. He would be my father-in-law if Elliot and I managed to work things out. I stared up at the other two elders. "All right, who knows the truth?"

Mason stepped forward, opening and closing his mouth as though he was fighting the need to tell me.

"Is my father still alive?" I asked, feeling the strain against my magic.

The elders were fighting the coercion of my truth spell.

"When was the last time anyone saw him?" I pressed.

Mason opened and closed his mouth again. "About... ten years ago. He... his wolf. I saw him." Mason grunted and shook his head as though he was shocked with what he was admitting to.

"Can he shift back?" I asked. "Is he stuck like everyone believes?"

Mason's eyes opened wide as he fought the coercion.

"Tell me!" I demanded.

Mason gasped, then exhaled in a huge rush, speaking fast. "No. He can't shift back. None of them can! I don't know if they're still alive. We don't know where they are now."

"So, you've seen all three of them?"

Mason nodded.

"And did they come back here for help?"

"Yes, but there was no way to communicate with them. Even in wolf form, we couldn't speak to them. There was a barrier between us."

My heart fell. "So, they came here for help, but you couldn't do anything about the curse?"

The effects of the spell were wearing off a lot faster than I'd hoped.

The elders were soon looking at each other with irritation and suspicion. They began to argue amongst themselves.

"I thought we weren't going to say anything about the cousins."

"I didn't! You did!"

I glanced over at Tommy and Jonah. "Time to go."

Jonah grabbed my hand and pulled me toward the exit, with the other three hot on our heels.

"What did you do to them?" Jonah asked, as soon as we broke through the doors.

"You put some sort of truth hex on them, yeah?" Darren asked, his eyes gleaming with excitement.

"You did great," Ruby said, smiling at me. "But damn, I miss my magic."

I stared at her, sadness in my heart. "It still hasn't come back?"

Ruby shrugged.

Darren reached out for her in comfort. "You aren't meant to be trying to use it yet."

"I haven't," Ruby admitted. "Not really, anyway. It's just... whenever I reach for the connection? It's not there anymore." Tears dashed down her cheeks and she brushed them away, forcing a smile onto her face. "It's silly, I'm sorry. It really doesn't matter. I have everything I need in you three," she said, referring to her Fated mates.

I doubt that very much. I didn't say it aloud. Magic was a part of us, the same way the shifter was a part of our men. I couldn't imagine that any one of them would be happy about having their wolves taken away from them. "I think we should get home," I said, reaching for Tommy.

"Whose home?" he asked.

I didn't know, but my head was throbbing. I put my hand to my temple and grimaced. "I don't care. I just need a minute to think."

Tommy grabbed my hand and pulled me into him.

I sagged against his strong body in relief as the pain began to overwhelm me.

"Let's go back to our place for a bit. You guys' want to come?" he asked the group.

Ruby shook her head in the negative. "I've got to catch up with Tiff later. We're organizing to speak to the witch's coven tomorrow."

I nodded, feeling dizzy. "Um, I think I need to lie down."

Tommy swept me up in his arms and started walking down the street, throwing the words, "Catch up with you guys later!" over his shoulder.

"I'm fine. Really," I told Tommy, though my eyes were already closing, and my head rested comfortably against his chest as we walked through town.

"You hold on. We'll be home soon," he promised, lending me his strength.

~

Tommy

"Is she okay?" Jonah asked me once we reached my place and got her sleeping form safely inside.

"I'm not sure," I said honestly. Glancing around our small house, I sniffed the air. Elliot had been here. I'd know that testosterone-fueled scent anywhere. I wasn't sure if he was still around, though.

I was just about to place a sleeping Bella onto the couch when Elliot's bedroom door flew open, and he marched out.

I squeezed Bella tight to me.

Jonah stepped in front of us protectively. "What do you want?" he asked, puffing up to face the Alpha.

Damn, I was proud of the pup. Even if together, we'd lose a fight to Elliot, every day of the week, I'd be glad to have my little brother standing by my side.

Strangely, Elliot looked perturbed by Jonah's aggression and actually took a step back.

There's a first time for everything.

"What's wrong with her? Is she hurt?" he asked.

The first phrase to jump to my mind was, 'what do you care?' but I bit my tongue and pulled out my adult voice instead. "I don't know. We went to talk to the elders about the Manterri cousins, and she fell asleep."

I moved over to the couch and gently lay her down, my shoulder killing me where it was still healing.

Jonah fussed over making sure she had a pillow under her head and pulled the throw blanket down over her.

I stood upright again.

Jonah stayed crouched on the ground, staring at our mate and stroking her face.

Elliot looked freshly showered, his skin still red from the heat and his hair wet. He looked thinner than he had a few days ago. So, he hadn't stopped to eat or drink anything.

The idiot. I stomped over to the fridge and started pulling out food and drinks. "Here." I threw him a bottle of sports drink and took out the fresh bread and roast turkey Mom had dropped over. "Make yourself a sandwich. You're no good to any of us if you starve your-self to death." I wasn't going to wait on the bastard, but he wasn't allowed to starve to death either.

"Thanks," Elliot said, shuffling over to the kitchen while drinking the blue sports drink.

I stepped back over to the couch and sat down on the end near Bella's feet. I reached out for her and touched her ankle, the skin cold between her long skirt and shoes. "Is she too cold, or is it just me?" I asked, unable to hide my concern.

Jonah put the back of his hand to her forehead as though checking for a fever. "She feels okay, but you're right. She is a little bit cold."

Elliot brought his plate over to the dining table, sat down, and began eating. "So, what happened?"

I sighed and crossed my arms over my chest. "We went to the council to ask them about Bella's dad, and the other Manterri cousins. The elders didn't want to divulge anything to Ruby or Bella."

"So, what did she do?" Elliot asked casually, almost in jest. "Put a spell on them or something?"

I shrugged. "Yeah. Pretty much."

Elliot froze, his mouth open and halfway to biting the sandwich. His gaze flicked to mine and connected. "Are you serious?"

I nodded. "But I don't think it agreed with her. She went all weak afterwards."

"What did she do to them?"

I ran a hand through my hair. "I don't really know. Darren said something about a truth spell."

Elliot took a bite of his sandwich, then shrugged, seemingly more at peace with the idea. "Fair enough, I guess. If they're hiding something, someone's got to make them tell the truth."

I swallowed down the need to tell Elliot what his dad had said. I'd never really talked to Elliot about the fact his parents were literally the only mated pair of wolves to officially sever their mating. It was generally unheard of. Divorce didn't exist in our community. But very occasionally there was a couple that couldn't sort out their differences and they officially dissolved their relationship.

Elliot's parents had been one of those rare couples, and since that day, Elliot's temper had been out of control. I'd never put those two facts together before, but now his anger made sense. As did his absolute doggedness about only marrying a Fated mate. Elliot had never once suggested he'd find a woman outside the pack to marry. *Never.*

"So, what did she manage to find out?" Elliot continued.

"Pretty much what they had assumed all along. Or at least what their mothers had. All three cousins had turned into their wolves and couldn't shift back. It's all linked to some curse that was set off by the High Warlock back then."

"And what are they going to do now?"

"We need to speak to the coven witches," Bella said, her voice a thready whisper from the couch.

I twisted toward her. "Hey! You're awake. Are you okay?"

She nodded and pushed herself to sit up. "I think I need to go home."

"Can't you stay here?" I asked hopefully, unwilling to be apart from her.

She shook her head, her gaze darting over to where Elliot sat, silent as a statue. "I think I did something wrong. That spell shouldn't have wiped me out. It was a simple spell to encourage the elders to just tell the truth. It's not even hard." She put a hand up to the bridge of her nose and closed her eyes. "But my head hurts. I think I need my mom."

"I'll drive her," Elliot said unexpectedly, standing up.

"No," I said, facing him. My black eye and swollen jaw had healed, but some of my cracked ribs were still sore, not to mention my shoulder. It wouldn't be fun to take another beating again, but I wasn't letting him anywhere near my mate alone.

"We'll all go," Jonah said.

I turned around as Bella staggered to her feet with Jonah's assistance.

"Don't fight," Bella pleaded weakly. "All three is fine."

"Jonah, take her to Elliot's car. It's the biggest." I turned to face Bella's third mate. "But *I'm* driving. And if I see even the smallest sign of you shifting, I'll stop the car and kick your ass to the curb. Got it?"

Elliot nodded. "Not a problem."

I frowned. *Giving in without a fight?* That wasn't like Elliot either. There was more to this change in his demeanor than he was letting on. "Fine, let's go."

We all got into Elliot's big truck. I drove, Elliot sat in the passenger seat, and Jonah was in the back cradling our mate tenderly, watching over her condition.

"Quickly please, Tommy," Bella whispered.

CHAPTER 18

ELLIOT

Sitting in the passenger seat of my own car while sober was a first.

"When'd you get back?" Tommy asked, his words clipped and short. He was still angry at me, and he had every right to be.

"About an hour before you got there," I said. I'd run all day and night, and then rested in some random forest almost a state away. I hadn't stopped to eat, and barely drank enough water to stave off dehydration. But I was back, now, and I had news. Though considering Bella's health, it was probably not the time to reveal all.

"And you're... okay?" Tommy asked.

A lump stuck in my throat. Even after what I'd done to him, he was still worried about me. "Yeah. You?"

He nodded. "All good."

I cleared my throat and prepared my apology. "I'm sorry I hurt you. No excuses. I was in the wrong." I'd heard ribs break. I'd seen blood. And yet the rage inside me had known no bounds. I'd hurt the one person who had stood by me my whole life. And if I didn't love Tommy the way I did, the shame of what I'd done last night probably would have driven me to just keep on running.

But my need to make amends—to check if he was okay—that was what brought me home. *And Bella, of course.* My shame on that front was intense as well. Enough to keep me away for a very long time.

Tommy shrugged. "Yeah, you were. But we're all good." His gaze flicked to the back of the car.

I twisted in my seat.

Bella had her head in Jonah's lap.

I swallowed hard against the self-disgust that rose, but I pushed down my damn pride and persevered. "I'm so sorry about yesterday, Bella. I shouldn't have lost control like that. It was unacceptable and I never wanted you to see me like that."

It was still early evening, so there was enough light in the car to see her face. She gazed up at me, meeting my gaze. "It's okay," she said, her voice a mere shadow of what it had been when we first met.

"It's not okay," I said, my chest tight with pain. "It makes me sick to think of it. I... was jealous. And fucking dumb. I don't know what else to say, except I'll make it up to you, somehow. I promise, Bella." And I would. I already had some ideas of how to do it.

Bella reached out and touched my arm. "You can't help how you feel, Elliot." Then she took her hand back.

The loss was as keen as a blade to my chest. There was no warmth in her touch. No tingle or awareness of me as her mate. I couldn't help how I felt? Did that mean she understood? Or just that she'd given up on me? I turned back and concentrated on the road in front of us.

Had I done irreparable damage to our connection with my jealousy last night? Or had Bella decided she was never going to forgive me? My stomach dropped and my throat tightened with grief. It was very clearly the wrong time to ask her if she still wanted me, but *God*, it hurt to think that one stupid mistake may have cost me my mate. *My only mate.*

"Almost there, Bella," Tommy said as he slowed the truck down and drove through the streets of the town.

I stared out the window. *Should I tell them all now what I found? Would it make Bella feel better?* Maybe she'd forgive me if I told her. "I met some wolves while I was running last night." The words fell into the quiet of the car like coins in a glass jar, shattering the silence.

"Who were they?" Jonah asked.

I turned around and stared at Bella. "I'm pretty sure I met the Manterri cousins last night. All three of them."

Bella's eyes widened, and even though she didn't try to sit up, a weak smile curled her lips. "Where? Where'd you see them?"

"Pretty much all the way over the state line. I got there last night and decided to turn back when I realized that I needed to come back and beg you to forgive me, rather than run away like some stupid kid."

Tommy snorted from the front seat.

Bella's smile lightened the pain in my heart.

It was hard being this honest. I stared at Bella. "You sure you aren't still casting a truth spell? I can't usually talk this much about my feelings."

She lifted her hand and twinkled her fingers. "Nothing left in the gas tank. Sorry. It's all you."

Somehow, I wasn't sure about that. *Maybe having a mate has its own magic?* I inhaled deeply, preparing myself to reveal all. "They were all gray in color. All of them were older, with whitening around their muzzles. And they were lean and dirty. Like they hadn't seen a good feed, or a shower, in a very long time."

Bella gasped.

The pained noise hit me in the gut. *Crap.* "I didn't mean it like that, I'm sorry. I've just been putting it all together in my head, and if they were any other wolf shifters, ones that flicked back to human often, they just wouldn't look like that."

"It's true," Jonah said, stroking her hair. "I think all Elliot's trying to say is that he thinks it could be your dad and his cousins, and not some other random pack." Jonah glared at me like I'd done something wrong, and to the young pup, I probably had.

I swallowed hard. "Exactly. I'm sorry if I'm not explaining this well. It's just... I wanted you to know that I think they're alive. And they're really out there."

"Where are they now?" Bella asked.

"I don't know. They wouldn't run with me, and I didn't know how to communicate with them. I stayed around for a while, but in the end, I had to leave, and they wouldn't come back with me." I'd tried to bring my mate's father home, and failed.

She closed her eyes. "At least they're still alive. Thank you, Elliot. It means a lot to me that you brought that home with you."

Tommy pulled the car to a stop.

I glanced outside at the little cottage-style house Bella lived in.

"Should I ring the doorbell, or..."

"No. Mom will know..." Bella said confidently.

Sure enough, the door burst open, and Bella's mom ran out, coming straight to the car.

Jonah opened the door.

Bella's mom pulled the door wider. "What happened?"

Bella smiled at her mom. "Hi Mom. I did a truth spell and it... I don't know."

"You did a truth spell on a wolf shifter?" Her mom gasped. "You can't do that! It screws with your magic."

Bella laughed softly. "Well, that's nice to know, now."

"I'll grab her," I said, getting out of the passenger door.. "Come here, beautiful." I reached for Bella.

She came into my arms willingly.

But once again, there was something missing. That *spark*, the instant connection I'd felt since the moment I met Bella. It wasn't there. Maybe it was because her magic was going haywire? Hopefully that was all it was.

"Bring her inside," Bella's mom said, waving madly at me and rushing ahead. "Put her on the couch and I'll make up a remedy." She darted inside the front door, purple skirts and orange ribbons flying in the breeze behind her.

"Your mom's... colorful," I said, smiling down at Bella to break the tension.

She smiled back, though it was weak. "She's eccentric, I know. But she's awesome."

Warmth pulsed through her words and envy panged in my heart. Bella loved her mom in a way that I'd stopped feeling about my own parents after the age of eight. I envied her that feeling. The ability to still admire her parent. Wanting to go home to her mom because she knew she'd be taken care of. I hadn't had that in a long time.

I rushed into the small house and placed Bella down on the couch amongst the fluffy cushions.

A sleek-looking black cat jumped up out of nowhere.

I stepped back, shuddering.

The cat opened its mouth, and through pointed teeth, hissed at me.

I couldn't help but laugh. "Um. Yeah. Nice to meet you, too."

Bella struggled into a seated position.

The cat walked over her legs, did a little circle, then sat down, glaring up at me.

I had to chuckle. "Is that cat a human you turned into a cat, or are all cats like that?"

Bella ran her hand down its black fur, and the cat arched into her caress. "Storm found us. She was meowing on our front step in the middle of the night. It was raining and she was completely drenched, the poor thing."

I sobered. "So, it was meant to be, huh?"

Bella nodded, and stared down at the cat, not looking at me. "Yeah."

Bella's mom rushed in and handed Bella a steaming beverage in a mug. "Drink this, slowly. It'll help replenish the magic you lost." She dusted off her hands and craned her head back to stare up at me. "You must be Elliot." She stuck her hand out

I shook it gently. "Yeah, I am. It's nice to meet you..."

"Kathy."

I inclined my head. "Nice to meet you, Kathy."

"Nice to meet you too. I saw you run off after Thanksgiving. Couldn't handle the competition, huh? Or...?" Bella's mom quirked an eyebrow at me.

Ouch. I couldn't help the answering smile that tugged at my lips. "I can see where Bella gets her strength from."

Kathy shrugged. "No shame in asking a question."

"True," I said, but I wasn't really interested in answering it.

"So," she said. "Is there any good reason why you left the other day?"

I thrust my hands into my jeans pockets and shook my head with a grimace of shame. "Nope. No good reason."

She cocked her head. "You're not dealing with the sharing part very well, are you?"

I rocked on my heels and shook my head again. "Nope. Not really."

She smiled. "It's good to see you can tell the truth. That'll serve you well. Now, I need to feed my daughter, then I'm going to put her to sleep for at least twelve hours. Then she should be good as new by tomorrow." She made a shooing motion with her hands. "So, all three of you. Out you go."

"Mom!" Bella complained, her eyes wide and annoyed as she stared at her mother.

"It's just one night, Bella. You need to recover properly. I'm sure your mates can survive without you for *one* night."

I managed to smile at Bella before Tommy, Jonah, and I were all unceremoniously ushered out the door.

Kathy waved us off. "It's Saturday tomorrow. No coming by before ten AM., got it?"

"Yes, ma'am," I said, waving back.

She shut the door.

Something inside of me shifted. A strange sort of peace stole through me. *Was that what it's like to have a mother who cares about you?* Someone who wasn't scared to go to bat for you, even against someone as big as, well, me. I got back in the truck and let Tommy drive us all the way home. Everything was going to be all right. *It had to be.*

As we got out of the truck, tiredness hit me like a steam train. I was definitely going to sleep well tonight.

We started walking up the drive to go inside.

"Can I crash on the couch tonight?" Jonah asked.

"Yeah, of course. Why?" Tommy asked.

I wondered the same question. Jonah had never stayed over before, and it wasn't like Tommy, and I were going to get into another fight. He didn't need to stick around to act as mediator or anything.

Jonah shrugged. "I feel like I should. And do you think we could put an extension on this house if I move in? Or do you think we should just build a bigger house somewhere else? Billy said that the four of them sleep in one bedroom, in one bed, but I can't imagine we'd be doing that."

I stopped walking and stared at the kid. "What are you talking about?"

Jonah frowned at me. "Logistics. Bella is our mate. More than likely, she'll come here and live with us, like Ruby did with her three mates. So, can we tack on an extra bedroom here for me?"

I glanced over at Tommy, who was staring at me, too. Tommy

and I had never thought we'd ever share our home with anyone. It was our bachelor pad. Small, and often incredibly messy. "Not sure. I've never thought about it. Tommy?"

Jonah rolled his eyes at me. "Of course, you've never thought about it. You never thought you'd have a mate at all, let alone one you'd have to share with two other guys."

"How do you know that?" I asked the pup.

Jonah snorted at me. "Because when I was a kid, you told me that you were either going to marry your Fated mate, or no-one at all. You were drunk and probably don't remember, but I do. So, I'll sleep on the couch tonight, but once Bella moves in, I'm sleeping next to her, too." Jonah went ahead, opened the front door, and headed inside— into our home.

Tommy and I stood staring, in shocked silence.

I turned and stared at Tommy. "When did he grow up?"

Tommy's smile grew bigger and bigger, until he was practically grinning at me. "I'm not sure but it looks like we've got another room mate." Tommy headed inside.

I stared off into the distance, toward the town where my mate was being healed and pampered by her mother.

CHAPTER 19

BELLA

My mom was beginning to get on my nerves. I'd woken up in my bed, in my bedroom, to find her sleeping on a mattress she'd conjured on the floor. Then she'd sat on the toilet and chatted to me while I was in the shower—just in case I fainted. And now she was hovering over me, when all I was doing was sitting on the couch reading a book.

"Mom. Please." I groaned. "You need to relax. I'm fine."

"You weren't fine last night, Bella. You came home a mess," she reminded me for the umpteenth time.

I released the pent-up tension in my throat, sighing loudly. "I know. I made a mistake. But I didn't realize that working a spell on a wolf shifter would be any different to a human, or another witch."

"There's lots you don't know, Bella," Mom said, sinking down onto the couch opposite me and staring at me the way she did sometimes. Like a teacher at school teaching me something as basic as my ABCs.

I rolled my eyes. *Heaven help me.* "Mom, don't patronize me. Please. I'm not one of those girls who runs around making all the normal mistakes you're meant to do when you're young. I do well at school, I've never slept with any boys, let alone had the chance to sleep around. I don't drink. I don't do drugs..."

"Yeah, yeah. Okay. I get it, Bella. Yes, you've been a dream child. I admit it." Mom put up her hands in defeat.

I sighed again. "I didn't mean it like that. I'm not perfect, far from it. But you don't need to helicopter over me like I'm two years old. I made a mistake and I'm reading all about it now." I held up the book I was reading which detailed the different strengths and changes to spells that were needed if a witch were to cast them on paranormal creatures. Shifters included.

Then a thought occurred to me, and I shut the book, careful to slide the ribbon bookmark into place before I lost my spot. "If putting a spell on a shifter takes a lot more energy and magic than most, because they burn through the magic faster, how do you think the High Warlock put a spell on the whole pack? Wouldn't that have like... killed him to do something that immense?" Especially since the curse continued to exist, far beyond his death...

Mom tapped her fingers against her lips in contemplation, her brow furrowing. "You know, I've never really thought about it."

"Probably because you didn't have confirmation that there was a spell cast."

And there *was* a hex on the pack, I was sure of it. If the High Warlock had gone to the trouble to tell the pack elders that he was punishing them for our moms' getting pregnant, then he definitely followed through with the curse.

"Bella," Mom said, staring at me. "We don't know what he—"

The doorbell rang.

"Well, we're about to find out, Mom."

The front door opened, and Ruby and Tiffany called out. "Hello?"

"Come on in," I answered.

Ruby walked into the room, eating a packet of chips while grinning at Tiffany. "You are *so* jealous. Stop denying it! I can see you glowing green from here."

"Jealous of what?" I asked, putting the book down and getting to my feet.

Mom jumped up too, following me and what I was doing.

"Jealous of us," Ruby said, crunching on another chip. "Tiff wants her mates, like *yesterday*."

Tiffany rolled her eyes as though Ruby was exaggerating, but then crossed her arms over her chest. "It's not like *that*."

I cocked my head. It kind of looked like it was, but I wasn't saying anything yet.

Ruby groaned. "It has to be! Why else wouldn't you come to Thanksgiving even though you were invited?"

"Your house is tiny, Ruby. As if you were going to fit more of us in when you already had ten."

"Tiny? Oh, my God... you're kidding me, right?" said Ruby, frowning.

"Are you guys ready to go?" I interjected. They'd obviously been fighting about this for a while, and it wasn't going anywhere. "What time did you say the Coven wanted us there, Ruby?"

Ruby gave Tiff the eye, then flicked her gaze back to me. "About ten."

I picked up my cell phone from the coffee table and checked the time. "We better get going then." I turned around and grabbed my house keys and my shoulder bag, slipping my purse and my cell into it. "See you later, Mom. I've got my phone if you need me."

Mom smiled and waved. "Make sure you watch your energy today. You'll feel drained if you do too much!"

"What happened yesterday?" Ruby asked.

I shuffled all of us out the door. "Tell you in a sec." As soon as I managed to shut the door behind me, I blew out a sigh of relief. I needed some space.

"So, what's going on?" Tiff asked as we walked along the garden path.

We all jumped in my car so I could drive us to the Coven meeting which was happening at the old church.

"Basically," I said, as I reversed out the driveway then put the car in gear, "I worked a truth spell on some of the wolf elders yesterday, and it kind of wiped me out."

"You okay now?" Ruby asked as we drove towards the church. "You did look pretty exhausted yesterday."

"What did I miss?" Tiff asked from the back seat.

Ruby turned around from the passenger's side. "We went to the wolf elders yesterday and demanded some answers about our dads. I messaged you about it, but you said you had to work."

"What did they say?" Tiff asked, her voice unusually high pitched.

I answered that one. "They said that the High Warlock told them that the punishment for getting our mothers pregnant was that the whole pack was going to die out."

"Yeah! And I thought that it wouldn't matter if no females were born to the pack this generation, because there's so many other wolf shifter packs around, the guys could just mate with them," Ruby added.

"But?" Tiff asked.

"But" I continued, "they said that none of the men who *have* married outside the pack have had children. None of them. No living children, anyway. So, if they stayed and mated with a woman from the pack, born before us, they only had sons. And if they marry outside the pack, even now, then they don't have any kids at all."

Tiffany grunted. "Well, that sucks."

I nodded, turning into the gravel parking lot by the church. "It's a very effective, but cruel and unconscionable punishment."

The High Warlock had known what he was doing in that regard. He must have *really* hated the wolf shifters.

I parked the car and turned off the engine. I wasn't sure whether to tell the girls about what Elliot had said last night about our fathers being alive just yet. Mostly because I wasn't sure about what I was going to do about Elliot and me, so the information he'd brought home seemed kind of tainted.

He also didn't seem like the kind of man to lie, so at some point I was going to have to tell Tiffany and Ruby that our fathers were more than likely alive but were trapped in their wolf form... forever. That was, unless we could work out a way to unravel the High Warlock's insanely intricate, and obviously powerful, curse. Either way, it was far too much to think about right at this minute. "Let's go," I said, grabbing my bag and hopping out of the car.

Together we walked into the old church, for our meeting with the Coven.

We were greeted by Simone, a young witch like us, but the daughter of the current High Warlock, and a powerful witch in her own right. "Hello Bella, Ruby, Tiffany. How can I help you three today?"

I smiled at her, though something about her voice grated on my nerves every time I saw her. "We have an appointment with the Coven."

Simone's eyebrows flickered a little, then she said, "Have a seat. I won't be long."

We glanced around. There were only two seats in the foyer, and we weren't about to sit down.

Simone went through the stained-glass doors and into the main area of the church where voices could be heard and people moving about.

"Are you sure they're going to see us?" I whispered to Ruby.

She nodded. "They better."

I could feel her energy vibrating around her and could have sworn I felt her magic pulse. *Didn't she say that her magic was gone?*

Simone popped back through the doors; a large, fake smile plastered on her face. "I'm sorry, but the High Council are too busy to speak to anyone today. Can you make another appointment for next week, perhaps?"

I glanced at Ruby, who was growing redder and tighter in the face, and Tiffany, whose flashing blue eyes were not a sign of serenity.

Uh-oh. "And when would the next available appointment be?" I asked, not wanting the fight my premonition knew was brewing. "It's kind of urgent."

Simone conjured a diary out of thin air and began flicking through the pages. "Well, you see, Tabitha is away next week with her family, and the week after that they're completely full."

Tiffany glared at me.

I tried to ignore her, even though her look felt like hot daggers stabbing into my cheek.

She stepped closer. "Do the thing," she whispered.

I pressed my lips into a thin line. I knew what Tiff wanted me to do. They'd made me use a freeze spell on our mothers on multiple occasions, and every time we'd gotten into more trouble than it had been worth. But to do it to Simone... the penalty would be *a lot* worse than being grounded for a month.

"If you don't do it, I will," Tiff whispered, lifting her hands.

"Fine," I said, rolling my eyes and conjuring the spell I was far too good at.

"Fine, what?" Simone asked, lifting her gaze to me.

I cast the spell over her, and she froze, that 'bored stupid' look etched into her pretty features.

Worry smacked me in the gut. "I'm going pay for that one. I can already tell."

"Then let's hurry," Tiffany said, gripping my arm and pulling me through the huge church doors and into the inner sanctum of our Coven elders.

The three of us stopped short.

The two witches and two warlocks that made up our high council were sitting around on couches casually drinking coffee and eating cake.

Tiffany turned to me. "Yeah, they're *so* busy they can't even speak to us. Can't you tell?" she hissed.

When the four members turned to us, shock was plastered all over their faces.

I drew my magic into me and flung out a protection spell around all three of us. I didn't know what was going to happen in the next hour, but my tingling premonition senses were on fire. "Don't move too far from me," I said to Tiff and Ruby. "Both of you."

My friends knew me well and nodded.

Together, we walked toward four of the most powerful beings in our town. There was no going back now.

CHAPTER 20

BELLA

I held my magic tight to me, curling protectively around Ruby, especially. Tiffany was a good witch. She could handle herself to a certain degree, but if they decided to attack? Ruby wouldn't stand a chance.

"What are you doing in here?" Tabitha asked, setting down her teacup and standing up. "Where's Simone?"

"Simone told us to come right in," Tiffany lied.

Tabitha frowned and her lips twitched.

Pressure against my protection spell made me gasp. *Who is trying to hurt us?*

David, the current High Warlock, stood up and approached us, his shoulder-length black hair more gray than black nowadays. "What do you three want?"

"I told you," Ruby said, "when I made the appointment. We want to talk about the old High Warlock."

"What about him?" Rose asked from the couch. She looked relaxed, plaiting and re-plaiting her long white hair.

"We want to know what he did to our fathers," Ruby said.

My heart thumped in my chest, adrenaline zinging through my bloodstream. Something had changed in the room.

"What are you talking about?" Rose asked, sounding exasperated. "How do you even know who your fathers are? Weren't they just some warlocks from up north?"

Tabitha's eyes had become guarded, her demeanor taking on an even more frosty feel. "The high warlock is gone girls, dead. He took his secrets with him."

I didn't believe that for one second. I stepped forward, unwilling and unable to let this go. "Our fathers were, or are, wolf shifters. The High Warlock cursed them when he found out our mothers were pregnant with us."

There was a round of gasps from the others, except for David and Tabitha.

David narrowed his eyes and stayed silent.

Tabitha glared at me. "Lies."

I swayed, wanting to take a step back, but unable to back down without compromising my protection spell. I grounded myself and stayed exactly where I was. "I don't think so," I said, "but you're right —we don't know if it was *him*, or someone *else* in the community. So, perhaps you can help us solve a riddle? You are, after all, the four most powerful members of the Coven." I injected as much light-heartedness and sincerity into what I was saying, as possible. After all, it was the truth.

Tabitha lifted her chin. "What riddle?"

"Well," I began, "the puzzle is this. If my mother had gotten angry at my father and forced him to shift into his wolf form, and he was never able to shift back, how could she have done such a thing to begin with, and how would we undo it?"

The room went silent, and David and Tabitha exchanged glances.

"Sounds like a transformative spell to me," Rose said from the couch. "Though, to keep it going for twenty-years or more, would require an extreme amount of grounding."

"Grounding?" I repeated. "What do you mean?"

Horus, the other warlock in the room who hadn't spoken yet, turned to look at me from where he sat on one of the other couches. "Grounding is where you base a spell. Generally, we ground most spells in our own magic. But it is possible to ground a spell in a place, or a person, or even an object. Though that thing, whatever you chose, would weaken over time—eventually."

"Could I ground a powerful spell in something like a book?" I asked. *Could it really be anything? And if it was, how were we going to find such a thing?*

Horus shook his head. "No. Grounding a spell requires something of extreme power, and magic in itself. So, to ground a spell for twenty years, it would need to be grounded into a younger person, or a place to last. Like this church, for instance. Something with consistent longevity." He gestured to the building around us.

"And what if that person died?" I asked.

Horus shook his head. "Then the spell would be released."

Ruby stepped up. "So, you're saying that if someone put a spell on our fathers that still exists to this day, then the spell is grounded by something equally powerful?"

Rose nodded. "Yes, most likely."

I nodded, thinking about the elements of the spell and how much power it would have sucked off the High Warlock.

"How would we break such a spell?" Ruby asked.

"You'd need to destroy the element that it is locked to," Tabitha said, lifting her chin. There was something strange about her, about the anger she displayed around this subject.

I narrowed my eyes and followed the feeling of my premonition. "You know what it is, don't you?" The hairs on the back of my neck stood up.

"I don't know what you're talking about," Tabitha said, sauntering back to the safety of the other coven members and standing behind the couches.

I took a small step closer. "I think you do. Is it all linked? The infertility? The plan to destroy them all?"

"What's she talking about, Tabitha?" Rose asked.

"Nothing," Tabitha hissed. "She doesn't know what she's saying."

I looked at Rose, who was still sitting on the couch. "Whatever spell the High Warlock performed on our mothers when they were pregnant with us, seems to have made the whole local wolf pack infertile in a way. There hasn't been a single live female born to the pack since the day the three of us were born."

"Good," Tabitha snorted. "I hope they die off."

"They will," Ruby practically shouted with fire in her eyes. "Without females, the blood lines will be lost!"

"Is it possible?" Horus asked the group, his face showing nothing but surprise. "I know the High Warlock hated the wolf shifters, but I never thought he'd do such a thing to an entire town of people…"

"Horus, shut up," Tabitha said, then rounded the couches and started flapping her hands at us. "You all need to go. Now."

"Not until you tell us how to free our fathers," I bit out, anger swelling in my heart. "We've been without them our whole lives already. It isn't fair."

Tabitha stopped a foot away from me and glared. "There's no way of knowing if they're even still alive."

They were. Elliot had seen them.

"It doesn't matter," I said. "Just tell us how to undo the spell."

Tabitha rolled her eyes and huffed.

"Please," Tiffany added, her gaze more imploring than angry.

I considered throwing a truth spell at the witch before me, but that would mean letting go of the protection spell around me and my friends, and I didn't trust Tabitha one bit.

"Fine," she said, stomping her foot. "I'll tell you if you leave, immediately."

"We will," Ruby said.

"I'm not talking to *you*, traitor," Tabitha all but spat at Ruby. "You're not welcome here any longer."

Ruby blinked and shut her mouth.

Tabitha's gaze zeroed in on me. "I can smell them on you too, Bella, so make your choices wisely. If you choose to marry a shifter, you will never be welcomed back into the Coven. Never."

I swallowed hard, not willing to even contemplate what she was saying. "Tell me what to do," I pressed.

"The High Warlock hated the wolf shifters," she said. "He was in love with a woman once, a witch in our town. They were set to be married, but then the woman ran off and mated with one of the wolf shifters. Had his pups, too."

I swallowed hard. "What's that got to do with me?" *Though that does sound like my grandparents, and Darren's.*

She continued, and there was a vicious gleam in her eyes that made my stomach churn. "So, when your mothers came to the High Warlock and told him they were all pregnant to a bunch of wolves, he cast a spell to bind you all together. As the three of you grow—the pack dies. The spell is grounded to your very lives. As long as you're all still living, your fathers will remain wolves, and the pack will die out. It's that simple."

Her words hit me like a full-blown storm, smack in the face. I gasped and staggered backwards, holding onto my best friends and letting go of the spell I was casting.

Ruby grabbed onto me.

Tiffany pressed in close. "It can't be," she said.

Simone barged in through the doors. "What are you three doing in here?"

"We're going. We're going," I said, groaning as my legs gave out beneath me. I would have fallen to the floor if Tiffany and Ruby hadn't caught me. *Damn. I've run out of power. And we are in danger.* I could feel it. Someone very close by wanted to cause us serious bodily harm.

"Tiff," I said. She was the only one with any powers left to rely on. "The hallowed ground beneath us will help boost your magic. Can you get us home?"

"Your place?" Tiff asked.

I nodded and closed my eyes.

Tiffany grabbed hold of us, and magic whirled around me, then we were all falling to the floor in my mom's lounge, the softness of the carpet and the rugs beneath my knees a heavenly feel after the coldness of the Coven's headquarters.

"Damn, that hurt." I groaned, holding my belly.

"Bella, is that you? What happened?" Mom raced out of the kitchen and fell to her knees in front of me. "Are you okay? Look at me."

I stared up at her. "I need some more... of that tea."

Mom stared around at all three of us and staggered to her feet. "You three, don't move. Just stay there. I'll be right back." Mom ran to the kitchen to make her brew.

I leaned to the side, resting my head on the couch and cradling my aching stomach.

"You okay, Bella?" Tiff asked.

I opened my eyes and stared at my best friend who was also on her ass on the carpet. *Damn, that took it out of me.* "Yeah, thanks for getting us out of there. I couldn't stay a minute longer." Not to mention the fact that I'd used up all my magic. If I'd needed to protect Ruby, or myself, I would have been defenseless.

Ruby was gasping like a landed fish and struggling to get up.

"Just stay down, Ruby," I said, flapping my hand. "It's nice down here."

Ruby continued to struggle until she was up and sitting on the couch.

"No. I need to get up." She groaned, then collapsed against the back support. "That's better."

"What's wrong?" I asked her. "You seem more exhausted than me."

Ruby had gone deathly white, and I wasn't sure if it was the shock of what we'd learnt about our fathers, or her petering magic. "I'm pregnant," Ruby whispered.

Tiff and I stared at each other, then both managed to get to our feet and stumble over to the couch to embrace our friend.

It hurt to get up, and it hurt even more to launch myself at Ruby, but once I was sitting down again, hugging her, everything relaxed.

"Congratulations," I said, though I couldn't even imagine what that must feel like for her.

Tears tracked down Ruby's pale face. "I only found out yesterday, and I just... I can't cope with all this." She threw her hands up in the air.

I looked at Tiff, then up at my mom as she walked into the room carrying a tray of mugs. "All of you need this."

I took mine and handed Ruby hers. "Is this safe for Ruby to drink, Mom?"

My mom's eyes widened. "What do you mean?"

Ruby sobbed, wiping the tears from her face. "I'm pregnant, and I don't want anything to happen to my babies."

My mom's mouth dropped open. Then she set the mugs down and pulled Ruby into her arms, where my friend cried and cried.

I took a long drink of my mom's tea, feeling the heat and the healing spreading through my body.

Mom stroked Ruby's hair and said, "Nothing's going to happen to your babies, Ruby. Believe you me."

I shook my head, still in disbelief. *Babies...* What was going to happen next?

CHAPTER 21
JONAH

I'd been busting to go see our mate from the moment we'd woken up, but Tommy convinced me to go for a run first. Then breakfast at Milly's, followed by a shower. By the time we were actually ready to go, it was almost eleven A.M. "For fuck's sake, Tommy. Hurry up!" I paced the lounge impatiently. "Or I'm going to leave without you."

"You have your own car, you know," Elliot said from the kitchen where he was eating a second—or was it a third?—breakfast.

I glared at him for being right. "Don't you ever stop eating?"

He laughed. "Not really."

"Thanks for the reminder I've got my own car." I charged for the front door.

Tommy came out of his bedroom just at that moment, his shirt still unbuttoned, and his shoes in hand. "Stop being such an old woman, Jonah. I'm coming."

I growled and shook my head. "Nope. Can't wait! See you there. I need to go." I ran out the door, jumped in my car, and took off. Everything in me this morning was buzzing with adrenalin and excitement. I could barely stay still. I'd slept on Tommy's and Elliot's couch, which hadn't been the best nights' sleep of my life, but I felt good this morning.

I felt alive, like I was *finally* where I was meant to be in my life. Maybe I was, now? I was meant to live with Tommy and Elliot, even if they hadn't come to realize it just yet. Without a thought I drove through town, turned into Bella's street, and barely managed to turn off the car engine before I was out and bolting for the front door.

It opened before I could knock, Kathy grinning at me. "I was expecting you at exactly 10:01."

I grinned back at her. "The other two convinced me to go for a run and eat first. Otherwise, I would have been here, believe me."

She glanced over my shoulder. "So, where are they now?"

"I left them at home. They were being way too slow."

Kathy laughed; the sound similar to Bella's. "I like your attitude, Jonah. Come in. They're all here."

I walked through the front door and into the lounge. "All...?" I queried.

And there they were. Five more witches.

My heart hammered in my chest. "Ah, good morning."

"Hey Jonah," Bella said, getting up from her place on the floor and coming over to greet me.

I grabbed her beautiful face and planted a kiss on her soft lips, enjoying the sweetness of her taste.

Then she turned back to her cousins.

I narrowed my eyes at the scene before me. "What are you guys up to?"

Ruby, Tiffany, and Bella were sitting on the floor, surrounded by books and crystals. While their mothers were sitting at a round dining table, also surrounded by a plethora of books. Empty cups of tea and mugs of coffee were strewn about the room.

"You look like you've been at it all night."

The women laughed.

"Not all night," answered Bella. "We had a break somewhere in the middle."

My mouth dropped open. "I was joking. Have you really been up all night?"

Bella settled back onto the floor amongst her nest of books. "We have. We're trying to find a way to undo the spell the High Warlock put on us."

I slid onto the couch, staring down at the three witches on the floor. "To you? I thought the spell was on the pack, and your fathers?"

Ruby screwed up her face. "Yeah, well, we went to the Coven yesterday and questioned them about what they knew."

That didn't sound so good. "And what did you find out?"

"Maybe we should wait until the others are here, too?" Tiffany said. "You don't want to repeat the story over and over."

I rolled my eyes. "They could be another hour. Bloody slowpokes."

Bella lit up. "Nope. They're just around the corner." She stood up and the sound of Elliot's truck hurtling down the street became obvious. Bella's breath hitched as she stared out the window and she bit on her lip as though nervous. Her eyes widened. "They're both here."

"Yeah. Why?" I asked, narrowing my eyes at the worry in her voice. "Haven't you and Elliot sorted your shit out yet?"

Bella smiled at me but didn't answer. Instead, she walked to the front door and opened it for their timely arrival.

I shook my head. "*I* didn't get a personal welcome."

Kathy laughed. "Yes, you did. I just beat Bella to the door."

I smiled at her. Was that a sign that Kathy liked me more than the other two? Or that Bella didn't like me as much? I wasn't sure I wanted to know at this point in time. Questions like those were laden with explosive possibilities like a minefield. It was probably best if the answers to such questions remained elusive and unspoken.

The guys came into the room and Elliot stood next to me. "We were one minute behind you."

I shrugged. "Only because I left when I did. You guys don't like being last."

They couldn't argue with the truth.

So, I turned back to the cluster of witches. "Bella was about to tell me about what the Coven said yesterday, but they wanted to wait for you guys. So, Bella?" I raised my eyebrows at my mate.

She smiled at me with a true, warm smile that made my heart leap. "The High Warlock hates wolf shifters because the woman he was in love with ended up married to a wolf shifter instead."

I frowned. "Do you mean...?"

Bella nodded. "Yeah, I'm pretty sure it's my grandparents on my dad's side, but let's leave that for the minute. The important part is that the witch we spoke to yesterday said that the whole spell, the pack being unable to have any more females, and our dads being wolves forever, it's all linked!"

"To what?" I asked.

Bella looked at Ruby, who stared at Tiffany. Then they all looked up at me, and the pain and intensity there was too strong to handle. "To us," they said as one.

Tommy slid onto the couch beside me, his hands curled into fists on his knees. "What do you mean, it's linked to you?"

Kathy stood up. "According to the witch the girls spoke to yesterday, and she isn't the most reliable source of information..."

"She's a nasty bitch, that one. Always has been," Sherie said, sitting at the table.

Kathy shrugged. "But if there's any truth to it at all, then we need to investigate how to unhook it."

"And if you unhook it, the spell might be broken?" I asked. "Would that mean the Manterri cousins might be able to shift back again?"

Bella nodded. "Yes, and the pack might have a chance of having daughters once more."

Elliot and Tommy looked at each other.

"That would change everything," said Elliot, speaking for them both.

I nodded. "It would. So, how can we help, ladies?"

Sherie stood up and stretched like a cat. "You can take the girls out for a walk into town. We need more tea, and they need a break."

"But Mom..." Bella started to say.

"No buts," Sherie said. "Ruby especially needs a break." She gave the girls a look that had them all standing and getting ready to go out.

"What's wrong with Ruby?" I asked, when no-one else looked as if they were going to question the logic. When again, no-one answered, I glanced at Ruby, and her gaze connected with mine. "Are you okay?" I pressed.

She nodded, though her cheeks were pink. "I'm pregnant."

My mouth dropped open, then a happy feeling washed over me. "Congratulations!"

"Another male shifter for the cause," Tommy said from beside me, a smile on his face. "Congratulations."

Ruby slid her hand to her belly. "I'm not sure it's going to be a boy."

I frowned at her. "It has to be, doesn't it? The spell isn't undone yet."

Ruby glanced at Bella, who looked at me. "It's too early to really be talking about it. She's only five weeks along. Let's go get some fresh air."

The six of us trundled outside and I managed to snag Bella's hand so I could walk beside her as we strolled toward the shops.

"Is Ruby okay?" I asked.

Bella nodded. "Yeah, but she's scared."

"Of what?"

Bella shrugged. "Of everything. Losing the baby. Of the sacrifice that may be needed to break the curse."

"The sacrifice?" I repeated, hoping I'd heard wrong.

Bella nodded. "Yeah. A lot of these very old, insanely powerful spells require a sacrifice to break the spell. And since the three of us are the ones linked to the spell, it's possible that if we gave up our lives, the spell would be broken."

My mouth dropped open. "No."

"It's true," Bella said.

I shook my head. "That's not what I meant. I'm sure it is true, but *no*. You can't do that. We just found you, Bella. I can't lose you, and Ruby's mates can't lose her either. It would kill us all."

Bella smiled. "Don't worry. I'm not intending on giving up my life anytime soon."

"I hope not," I said. "You've got too much to live for. We all do now." Bella had given my life purpose, and I intended to see us both through to a ripe old age.

We turned the corner and began weaving through the townspeople who walked up and down the street on their daily errands.

Bella turned to me. "Tiffany is starting to get a bit impatient about finding her mates. Is there any way we can introduce her to some of the men in your pack? Do you have... socials? Or something like that?"

I grinned at her. "She should just hang around Milly's for a few days. We *all* go there. If her mates are part of our pack, then she'll see them one day or the next."

Bella smiled. "That's not a bad idea. Thanks."

Elliot

"Wʜᴀᴛ's ᴡʀᴏɴɢ ᴡɪᴛʜ ʏᴏᴜ?" Tiffany asked me.

I stared at my mate and ignored the cute blonde. I sighed. "I need to go talk to Bella. Do you mind?"

She shrugged. "Not at all. Send Jonah to me so I have someone to talk to."

"Not a problem." I strolled over to where Jonah and Bella were chatting and smiling happily.

They turned toward me.

Bella's smile died, like a light inside of her was switched off.

Fuck. "Hey Jonah. Can I talk to Bella for a bit?"

Jonah stared at Bella.

She nodded as though giving him permission to leave her.

"Tiffany wanted you to go talk to her," I told him.

Jonah nodded and slunk away.

I wandered a bit further away from the group.

Bella followed me.

I knew that my wolf shifter brothers would likely be able to hear us, no matter how far I walked. "Hey," I began. "I just wanted to talk to you about yesterday."

Bella nodded, and kept her gaze on me, but didn't say anything.

I swallowed hard, pushing forward, despite how uncomfortable I was. "I can feel a... shift in how you feel about me. So, I just wanted to apologize again. Make sure you know that it won't happen again."

Her lips twisted in a strange smirk that made my gut sink. She didn't believe me. When she raised her gaze to mine, my heart dropped. "I don't think you can promise that" she said. "You're an Alpha. You're like... an Alpha's *Alpha.* You aren't meant to share a mate. You're meant to have your own."

I swallowed hard, forcing the lump in my throat down so I could speak. "I don't have another mate, Bella. You're it. Fate doesn't make these mistakes." That was what I'd come to realize. I'd been waiting for my Fated Mate, and I'd found her. So, what if she loved Jonah and Tommy as well? As long as she loved me, nothing else ultimately mattered.

She shook her head, glancing away. "Elliot, I think we should cut this... connection we have as soon as possible. It'll only get more painful, the longer we're together."

I froze, afraid to move. "Bella, what do you mean?"

She stared at the concrete and scuffed her shoes against the pavement. "I mean, we've only kissed once. You should be able to walk away from all of this relatively easily."

"Walk away?" I repeated. *Is she serious?*

She nodded. "I mean, you shouldn't have to share your mate, and it's obvious I'm not the right person for you. I'm quiet. I'm not nearly strong enough to handle someone with your strength—your possessive nature." She lifted her gaze long enough to look at me. Then as tears glimmered in her eyes, she looked away again.

"You don't mean that," I said. "You're, by definition, perfect for me, Bella." It hurt to admit that I *knew* she was perfect for me when I'd acted so poorly, almost as much as it hurt to hear her reject me.

She threw her head back and flicked her hair over her shoulder. "I can't do this, Elliot. You scare me. Your wolf. You. All of it. I can't handle you. I'm sorry."

A growl rose in my chest, and I pushed it down. "But you can handle Jonah and Tommy? Is that right? I'm too much for you, but they're *just* right? Like this is some kind of Goldilocks and the three bears porridge scenario?" Anger boiled inside me.

Bella sighed and shook her head, "See? You can't even acknowledge that the other two suit me better. It's obvious you can't change, so let's just stop pretending I'm right for you. You need someone so much better than me, Elliot. Stronger. Sexier..." She stopped midsentence, putting a hand to her head as though she had a sudden headache.

I reached for her, but she flinched, and I took my hand back.

"Bella, please, I..." I wasn't sure what I was going to say next, but a strange sort of wind swept through the town. I inhaled sharply, a shiver of unease working its way down my throat. "Do you feel that?" I asked.

I glanced toward Tommy and Jonah just as the girls began to faint, falling toward the pavement.

All three of us dove simultaneously to save each of them from hurting themselves.

"What the hell...?" Bella drooped, and her knees seemed to give way because she was soon tumbling to the ground.

I reached out and grabbed her up into my arms, awkwardly pulling her limp body against me.

Tommy swung Ruby up into his arms carefully.

And Jonah pulled Tiffany's unconscious form into his embrace.

I leaned down toward Bella's face where her eyes were closed, and her mouth was open. Her breath fanned my cheek.

"She's still breathing," I said aloud with relief, even as panic pushed through me.

Tommy growled, deep in his chest. "We need to get them back to their moms. *Now.*"

"Now?" I repeated, confused and terrified all at once which was an extremely unfamiliar feeling for me. Then I glanced up into the sky where a brewing darkness was beginning to gather. "Oh, fuck. That ain't natural."

"Let's go," Tommy yelled above the wind that had begun to howl like it had a mind and will of its own.

We ran for it, all three of us carrying a witch, through the main street where people ducked for cover, around the corner and down the street that would lead us back to Bella's house.

I was at the head of the group, carrying our precious cargo. When I glanced back, Tommy was right behind me with a pregnant Ruby and Jonah was a ways back. I'd have to help him with Tiffany.

Ahead, all three moms stood on the nature strip outside Bella's house, glancing from side to side, looking as terrified as I felt.

They ran toward us as we bolted to them.

"What happened?" Sherie cried, reaching out for Ruby.

"Let's get inside," I said raising my voice to be heard, pushing around the mothers. "Jonah needs help with Tiffany and the storm is about to hit."

The girls' moms went to help Jonah as lightning cracked in the sky above our heads, lighting up the whole town.

People screamed in fear and ran for their houses.

I pushed at the front door with my shoulder and went straight to the couches.

"I'm calling Jackson," Tommy said, placing Ruby carefully down on the couch nearest to him, then pulling out his cell. "He's going to want get here—and fast." Tommy walked away to call Ruby's triad.

I sat down with Bella in my lap and pulled her close.

Kathy dropped down in front of me and reached for her daughter's face. "Elliot, what happened?"

"We don't know. We were walking along the street. Bella and I were talking about, well, us. She put her hand to her head like she was experiencing a headache, then they all just passed out."

Kathy's eyes widened. "All of them? At the same time?"

I nodded. "Yeah, pretty much."

Kathy pushed to her feet and the mothers converged, whispering fiercely to each other.

"Hey!" I yelled, anger getting the better of me. "What's going on? What's happened to them?"

The mothers spun around to look at me.

Jonah was still holding Tiffany.

Her mom directed him to lay her down on the couch.

Kathy stepped forward; her brow furrowed. "We think it's the curse."

Thunder boomed over the house and the women jumped.

"What do you mean?" Jonah asked. "What's the curse doing now? Hasn't it taken enough from us?"

I nodded. *Yeah, especially our pack.*

Kathy's lips trembled as Sherie walked forward, dropping down in front of Ruby. "Ruby's pregnant with a girl."

"That's not possible, is it?" Tommy asked, back from speaking with Jackson. "They're on their way."

Kathy shivered. "The girls, Ruby included, are in essence.... the spell. The rules don't apply to them the same way they do everyone else. It's a magical loophole of sorts." She stopped and took a breath. "I believe that Ruby's baby will break the curse, if we can just keep her alive long enough to see her daughter born."

"So, what's wrong with them? Why are they all unconscious?" I asked, still not understanding what she was talking about.

"The curse is fighting back against the loophole," Rebecca said, checking on her daughter. "The spell doesn't want to be broken. All their lives are linked to it It only exists because of *them*... So, if we can't find a way to unhook it, their lives will be forfeit."

TOMMY

I walked over to where my best friend held our mate and put a hand to her head. "She's cold." Worry lanced through me.

Elliot growled. "Jonah, can you take her for me?" He stood up with Bella still in his arms.

Jonah sat down on the couch, accepting Bella's sleeping form into his care.

Then Elliot, the big idiot who Bella had been breaking up with when she fainted, began to strip off his shirt.

"What are you doing?" Kathy asked, staring at the huge form of Elliot's naked back.

Elliot twisted around to look at me, his eyes already shifting to his inner wolf. "I've got to do something. I can't stand around here and do nothing."

I didn't bother reiterating to him that Bella had technically already broken up with him.

Elliot wasn't going to let her go without a fight, and Bella didn't know Elliot well enough to understand just how stubborn he could be.

"Where are you going?" I asked, before he lost the ability to talk.

"I'm going to find the Manterri's…" Elliot said, as his teeth became pointed and garbled his speech. White fur sprouted through his skin, and he dropped to all fours to let the shift completely take him over.

"I'll get the door," I said, charging for the front door to let Elliot out, before one of the witches tried to stop him. The gale force winds hit me in the face when I opened the door.

But Elliot ran straight through the doorway and into the roiling storm.

Rain pelted down and, as I watched my friend disappear, my heart squeezed tightly in my chest. He may be a stubborn idiot, and I may owe him a beating, but *damn*, I couldn't imagine living my life without him around. I shut the door and turned back to the group.

All three moms stared at me like I'd lost my mind.

"Did he just say he was going looking for the Manterri's?" Kathy whispered.

I nodded. "Didn't Bella tell you?"

Kathy shook her head.

I sighed. "When Elliot went running the other night," *after losing his shit because he found us with Bella,* "he found the cousins. All three of them."

"They're alive?" Rebecca whispered, her hand straying to her heart and pressing against her breast.

I nodded. "We think so. Elliot said they wouldn't come back with him, but it looks like he's going to give it a second try."

The three older witches grabbed each other for support, staggering into nearby chairs.

Kathy lifted her hand and swung it around, clearing all the books off the floor and table.

"That's handy," I muttered. "Our house would always be clean, if we could do that."

Kathy ignored me. "We need to find a way to lift this spell."

The front door banged wide open and three wet, black wolves ran into the room.

I bolted for the front door and locked it shut this time as we weren't expecting anyone else that I was aware of. When I got back to the room, Jackson, Billy, and Darren were standing naked and wet in the lounge room.

"How is she?" they asked together.

"For goodness' sake," Sherie said, flicking her hand and magicking up three sets of jeans and black t-shirts for the guys.

"Thanks," Darren said, while Billy and Jackson went straight for their mate.

The storm brewed overhead, and the sparkling power of the lightning above lit up the sky.

~

Elliot

I RAN THROUGH THE TOWN, rain pelting my fur as thunder rolled through the sky. I was terrified—more so than I'd ever been in my entire life. My mate's life was in danger, and I was so afraid of losing her I couldn't even think straight.

Bella was my only mate. I'd never get another if she died. She was my only hope for happiness. Even if that hope was a tiny flame flickering hopelessly in the dark, especially after what I'd done so far to ruin her trust.

As I ran past the edges of the town, the storm cleared as though it had never been. The sky above my head became blue. The sun shone and the wind died down. I stopped running, my fur dripping wet, my eyes barely able to open from the sting of the wind. I shook myself, taking stock of my body. I had enough food in my gut, and a good sleep last night, I could run all day and reach the border by nightfall. It would hurt, but I could do it.

This time it wasn't anger driving me; it was pure panic. And a love that had grown with every minute since the moment I'd met my mate. Even if she wanted nothing to do with me after this, she couldn't die. I couldn't exist in a world where she wasn't.

I took the road around the next town, careful to dodge the city folk and took to running through the forests. I passed over the countryside, meeting cattle that leapt out of my path, and smaller, normal wolves who glared at me as I ran past. I didn't stop though my legs burned, desperate for rest. I kept my eyes peeled for danger and looked for any signs of the cousins I'd met just the other day.

I had no hope of helping Bella or her witchy cousins. I was no use to them where magic was involved. But I could find their fathers. I could bring them home. Maybe then the witches would have a chance of breaking the spell that held the Manterri's hostage in their own shifter bodies.

I ran long past the noon sun, watching it disappear on the horizon; stopping only briefly by a watering hole for some fresh water. Lapping it up with frantic gusto to soothe my parched throat. Then I kept moving. When night finally came, I was grateful for the dark, and the cold. My coat was drenched with sweat and the night air allowed me time to cool down.

There wasn't too far to go now. Last time I'd found the cousins, they'd been hanging around near the border. When I reached the state line, I slowed down to a trot and began to look for signs of wolf shifters. My heart pounded in my chest and my legs shook with sheer exhaustion, but I was nowhere near done with my quest. I wasn't going home without them.

The pack joked that I was an Alpha's *Alpha*. I'd never liked the responsibility of such a title and knew that when it came to our current pack dynamics, I'd never be called upon to do what a true Alpha would have done in the past. But I understood what it meant. I could command the respect of anyone in our pack. Those older than me. Those younger. The Alphas, the Betas, the Council and even the elders.

I'd never used my true power before, but one of the Manterri cousins had been Alpha-born, himself. And while the other two may follow me out of pure instinct, an Alpha wouldn't. Not unless I pushed the issue, which for the first time in my life, I might need to.

I lifted my nose and sniffed the air, catching the slightest scent of a wolf to the north. I took off running, jumping over logs and bolting around trees like my life depended on it.

When I finally found them, they were curled up around an old fire some human had stupidly forgotten to put out. The embers still glowed red and orange.

The largest of the three gray wolves got to his feet and growled at me.

I let go of my wolf, shifting back into human form. Staggering sideways under heavy fatigue, I finally collapsed to the ground beside the fire. The embers gave off only a small amount of heat. I put a hand to my aching stomach. "Fuck, I'm starving." *And cold.* I crawled over to the fire, rearranging the embers and sticking some dry wood onto the pile. The fire began to crackle and burn, lighting up once more.

I couldn't hear it, but I almost sensed the sigh in the other three wolves.

They moved closer, settling around me.

I leaned back against my hands and took a moment to catch my breath. I'd found them, and the relief was immense.

All three gray wolves were starved, their ribs protruding against their fur.

None of us really enjoyed eating in wolf form. It meant hunting down a live animal, killing it, and devouring it while still warm. We were taught as kids how to do it, as part of survival training. But it wasn't a preference and it wasn't fun. No wonder these guys were as thin as they were. They probably only ate the bare minimum amount of food necessary to stay alive. It looked like they were barely hanging on.

The fire began to crackle, and I reached forward to stir it up once more.

The wolves shuffled closer to me, tightening the circle around me, keeping me warm where the fire lacked.

I smiled at them. "Thanks."

They didn't respond, and I didn't expect them to.

Some wolves could communicate in a telepathic sense, but only members of a pack that ran together often. Brothers, sometimes, but not always.

I could imagine these three would read each other very well, especially after decades of being together—of being each other's only companions.

When I'd rested enough that my heart was no longer racing, the sweat had dried, and my legs no longer trembled, I pulled myself up so that I was seated to talk to them. They should be able to understand me. Unless they'd lost that sense too. "I'm Elliot Turnbridge. My father is elder Tony Turnbridge."

The largest of the gray wolves lifted his head and stared at me.

"My Fated Mate is Bella Swatch."

Another smaller gray wolf stuck his head up.

I turned to him. "You're Matthew Manterri?" He was Bella's dad, and half warlock. I looked at the largest of the three. "And you're Lucas?" Then at the final wolf. "Thomas."

The three of them stared at me, unmoving, barely breathing.

I could feel the tension within them. "I've come to ask you to come home. Back to the pack."

The wolves all stood up and began to turn away, their heads down, defeated.

I jumped to my feet. "Your daughters are all in grave danger."

They stopped.

"Yes, your daughters! You didn't know that Kathy and Rebecca and Sherie were pregnant, but they were. They gave birth to three daughters, all on Halloween."

The wolves turned to stare at me, unmoving. Focused. Listening.

My chest ached with pain at the thought of Bella at home, unconscious. "The girls are in real trouble. The curse that forced you three to remain wolf shifters forever is hurting them, and without you, I don't think their moms will be able to work out how to fix it."

There was a strange growl and a rumble, the men talking to each other in low-pitched wolf talk.

"I don't know if you can even go back to the pack. Or why you've stayed away this long. But if you can come back with me, you have to. You're the only lead we have."

The Alpha wolf began to turn away.

I let go of my humanity and shifted, letting my huge white wolf take over, allowing the anger to roll over my body and light me up from the inside. I growled loudly, standing over the Alpha and snarling. *You will come back. You will. For your daughters. And for yourselves.*

The two Betas bowed their heads, growling as they were forced to submit.

A small part of me hated having to do this, but a larger part reveled in being able to do something to help my mate. No matter the cost to myself or to my humanity. I'd gladly pay the price and have no regrets.

I growled harder, forcing the Alpha to do as I wanted—what my mate needed. Why they wouldn't come back, I didn't know. And quite frankly I didn't fucking care. Bella and her friends had grown up without their fathers and these men had lost half their lives. For whatever reasons they'd stayed away, I was sure we could fix it. Somehow. Someway. We had to.

The Alpha's head dropped in a show of aggression.

I snapped my jaws, feeling my heart pump and saliva pool in my gums. I didn't want to fight this wolf. He was weak. He was old. And he was one of my own. So, I dropped my head, made eye contact with the Alpha, and let the last thoughts go free. *Come back with me. Follow me now. If you don't, I will come back. And I will make you.*

I turned tail and started running home.

CHAPTER 23
TOMMY

The girls became red and started sweating around dinner time.

We took their temperature and all three were burning up at over one hundred and two degrees.

The moms panicked and called in other members of the Coven. They all hunched around the dining table, surrounded by books and herbs, spells, and crystals. There were witches and warlocks *everywhere*.

I sat quietly on the couch next to where Bella lay, watching over her.

"Do you think they're going to find the way out of this?" Jackson asked me from where he knelt on the floor, stroking Ruby's flushed face with a cool cloth.

The storm hadn't let up, and the rain was causing flooding in some of the houses around us. Only the magic of the Coven at the table in front of us kept this house safe.

"I wish we could just pick them up and take them home," I said in response, sighing with frustration. "Maybe they'd be safer with the pack?"

Jackson shook his head. "I don't understand any of this, so I'm just going to sit here and do as I'm told."

"You?" I huffed, almost laughing. "Since when? You're an Alpha, yourself."

Jackson was every bit as much of an Alpha as I was. Taking orders was not one of our fortes. But then neither was sitting back and just waiting for someone else to act. Jackson chuckled. "Since Ruby almost killed herself undoing the Halloween love spell. If it wasn't for us—hang on a second. Hey, Sherie!"

Ruby's mom looked up from the book she was studying. "Yeah?"

Jackson jumped to his feet, potentially onto something. "Could you use us to save the girls, like you did last time? They way you did on Halloween?"

Sherie pulled her glasses off her nose and stared at him in thought. "I suppose we could try. But Tiffany doesn't have any mates to draw strength from, Bella only has two here, and Ruby's pregnant. It's dangerous."

"Yeah, and so's sitting here waiting to see what happens," Jackson grumbled back.

"You could try Bella first," I said. "Jonah and I are up for *anything* that could bring Bella back." I glanced over at my brother who nodded.

Kathy looked at us. "But we need more than to just wake them up. We need to know what put them under in the first place. And who did it? I'm convinced someone who is still alive is pulling the strings on this spell. It's not simply the doing of the old High Warlock."

"Then who is it?" I asked.

"I bet you it's one of the High Council," Kathy said, grimacing as though angry.

"Like who?" Sherie asked. "Tabitha? I know she's a bitch, but do you really think she'd do this to our daughters?"

Kathy threw her hands in the air. "The High Council hate the wolf shifters, so why wouldn't they? Our daughters are making sure the pack line continues. The girls being Fated Mates with the pack boys is a nightmare for all those that want the shifter lines to fail."

I paced to the window and stared out; my brow bowed in confusion. "Why is it raining like this? Is it part of the spell? Or are they trying to stop us from leaving?" I turned back to the table of witches.

None of the strangers spoke.

Rebecca started to frantically flip through one of the books. "If the girls are being hexed, then perhaps we can protect them. There's a home enchantment spell that I saw earlier. It might not help Tiffany and Ruby but might bring Bella out of it. Here." She tapped a page and turned it toward Kathy.

Kathy swallowed. "I could try it, I suppose, but I'm not sure what good it will do to have Bella awake and not the others?"

It would help me.

Rebecca pushed the book over to where Kathy sat. "It will tell us if there's an external influence cursing the girls. If the protection charm wakes Bella, then we know it's coming from far away. If it doesn't, there's something internal going on here."

Kathy nodded and stood up, taking the book and going to stand in a strange spot near the kitchen.

"What's she doing?" I asked no-one in particular.

"Just finding the center of the house," Rebecca answered. "She'll create a shell of sorts that can cocoon everyone inside and hopefully stop whatever curse is hitting the girls."

"So, like a shield?" Darren queried.

"Exactly," Rebecca said.

Kathy began to read, to speak in a language I didn't understand.

The wind whirled around us, and the strangest, coldest sense of calm came over me. I sank to the couch, reaching out to hold Bella's hand.

Her skin felt warmer than it had been before.

"I think it's working," I said, breathless, not wanting to jinx it, but unable to keep the thought inside my head.

"Bella?" Jonah stroked her face. "Can you hear us?"

She rolled her head from side to side.

The woman behind us gasped.

I echoed the sound, happiness squeezing my chest. "Bella!"

Her eyelids flickered and slowly, too slowly, her eyes began to open. She saw me and frowned. "What happened?"

Thank you, God.

She tried to sit up.

Kathy rushed over to help us prop her up.

"Where's Tiffany and Ruby?" Bella asked. "Oh no, they're still there."

"Still where?" Jonah asked.

Bella turned around and stared at us. "The void. I left them in the void!"

Kathy reached out to touch her daughter. "What are you talking about, Bella?"

Bella put a hand to her head and turned so that she could slip her legs off the couch and put her feet on solid ground. "I can't explain it except that, there was nothing there. It was like a black room. We were all trapped there together. And we were just talking, waiting."

"A consciousness trap," Rebecca said with instant disgust and anger.

"A what?" I asked.

Bella sighed, rubbing her head. "It's a spell that collects your mind and traps it in a place your body can't reach. It's a complicated, very complex spell. Only a senior witch or warlock could perform it successfully."

Jackson slammed his fist into the opposite hand. "We need to find this bastard and put them out of their misery."

He was right. We needed to do something, and Jackson and I could rip apart a warlock. No problem. I turned to Kathy. "I assume you need to stay here to protect Bella, but where do we find the person who's doing this to them?"

Rebecca and Sherie stood up.

"They'll be at the church. There's nowhere else in town that has enough power to bolster a witch like this," Kathy said.

"And the rain?" I asked. "What's with the storm?"

Rebecca shook her head. "I don't know. I have to assume it's either a side effect of the dark magic, or it's an attempt to stop people trying to find her or him."

I grinned. "Luckily, wolves don't mind water."

Jackson cracked his knuckles. "I'm going with you."

"We are, too," Jonah and Billy said, jumping up. *My brothers.*

I turned to them and shook my head. "You need to stay here and look after everyone."

Jonah sulked.

Billy glared at me. "This is my mate's life too, Tommy."

"I know." I sighed and dropped my voice. "And if we don't make it back, it'll be your job to protect them, do you understand?"

Billy's eyes softened. "Fine."

"We're coming, too," Rebecca and Sherie said, stepping up as the Betas slunk away. "You're going to need the protection."

"Protection?" I asked, raising an eyebrow. "Jackson and I are both Alphas." We were the strongest of our pack. *Surely, we'd be capable of taking out a couple of distracted witches?*

Rebecca rolled her eyes. "I'm not talking about physical strength, boys. This witch is going to have a guard, and they will hurt you if they can. Kill you even if you get close enough. Sherie and I will keep a shield up so you can attack. We need to take them down before they kill our daughters."

Sherie shuddered. "Consciousness traps are dangerous. People go into them, and sometimes never come out."

"Never?" Jackson asked, glancing at Ruby with worry.

"Or if they do," Rebecca continued, "they're not sure which is the real world, and lose their minds anyway."

I clenched my teeth. "How long have they got?"

Rebecca exhaled sharply. "A few days at most."

"Then we haven't got a moment to lose. Let's go." I hurried to the front door and pulled off my shirt. "I hope you two have hurricane-ready umbrellas."

Rebecca and Sherie glanced at each other; determination written all over their tense faces. "Oh, we do."

Bella called out to me. "Tommy, please be careful!" She hadn't gotten up off the couch yet but was holding her hand out to me.

I couldn't stop myself from hurrying back to her, leaning down, and planting a kiss on her pouting lips. I cupped her cheek.

She looked pale and wan, but she was alive.

"You stay here, beautiful. I'll be back soon."

Bella's lip quivered. "What will I do if something happens to you?"

I chuckled. "Nothing will. Haven't you seen my reinforcements?" I pointed my thumb at Jackson and the two moms behind me.

Tears shimmered in Bella's eyes, but she nodded. "Please be careful. It's obvious these people will stop at nothing to tear us apart." Bella glanced around, alarmed. "Where's Elliot? He should go with you."

I grinned down at her. "Elliot left hours ago."

Bella frowned.

"He left?" She sighed and nodded so sadly it broke my heart. "Yeah. It makes sense. I told him that we shouldn't be together anymore. Of course, he left."

I shook my head. "That wasn't the reason, sweetheart. He's gone to find your dads and bring them home."

Her lips parted in a silent gasp, her eyes widening as though she couldn't believe what I'd just said. "I..."

I chuckled. "I've been friends with that knucklehead my whole life and I can tell you with certainty, he loves you. He's just having a hard time processing it all. I know you think it might be easier with just you and me and Jonah, but don't give up on him yet, yeah?"

Bella bit her lip, the unshed tears that had been swimming in her eyes spilling over and cascading down her cheeks. "Okay," she agreed.

"Good girl. Now..." I turned around and headed back to the front door, unbuckling my jeans and kicking off my shoes. "We're got an evil witch to take down."

"Or warlock," Sherie reminded me. "It could be anyone."

Jackson pulled off the black tank Sherie had magicked on him and rolled his shoulders and cracked his neck.

I nodded once. "Ready?"

He grunted in agreement.

I unlocked the front door, opening it a crack, then the wind banged it open in my face. I heard the exclamations of shock from the other witches in the room behind us but chose to ignore them and focus on what needed to be done. They could bolt the door again after we left. "Let's do it."

Together, Jackson and I shifted into our wolves and bounded out the front door and into the storm. Sherie and Rebecca were right behind us and, as I jumped down onto the road where the water was up to my shoulders, the need for the witches became suddenly apparent. I wasn't doggy paddling all the way to the church. If we couldn't run there, there was no point in being a wolf.

I was just about to shift back to human and start wading through what would be waist-deep water, when the river ahead of us running down the street, split like Moses and the Red Sea. I glanced back at the witches who were behind us.

Their arms were out, and their bodies were glowing like jewels of power.

I looked at Jackson, whose wolfy grin would have made me laugh if the circumstances weren't so dire. We had our way. *Time to go.* We took off, the witch moms at our backs and the road ahead of us clear. I didn't know what was going to happen, or if we were going to make it home again. But while we still had breath in our lungs, and our mates were at risk, I was going to fight for them.

I smiled as I ran through the streets, rain falling on us from above as thunder rolled across the sky. I'd never really given thought to the many reasons Bella had more than one mate, but for the first time, I was actually grateful for the fact.

Elliot was off conquering the cursed fathers.

I was here fighting the witches,

And Jonah was keeping our mate happy and safe at home.

Overall, I'd say we had all our bases covered. I just had to stay alive long enough to tell Bella I was happy about the fact she had all three of us.

I ran through the empty streets, bolting through the rain, adrenaline pumping in my veins as Jackson and I made our way to the old church. How Sherie and Rebecca kept up with us, I didn't know. I had to assume they were traveling by magic.

When we finally reached the road that led up to the church, we slowed down and glanced back to find the witches right behind us. We'd finally cleared the areas where tsunami levels of rain were falling, and the moms were using their magic to create shield-like-umbrellas over us all for the drizzle that remained.

I shifted back, ignoring the fact that I was naked. It was more important that we spoke to the witches and organized a plan than wasted time worrying about their supposed modesty issues. "So, what's the plan? Where will they be?" I had to shout to be heard above the wind and the thunder that still assaulted the world around us.

Jackson shifted back too.

Sherie didn't bother covering us, as I was pretty sure she knew we'd be back in wolf mode pretty soon. "There will be at least two of them, witches or warlocks. One conducting the spell, the other protecting them. There may be more. An army of protectors even. We really have no idea how deep this runs until we're facing it head on."

"So, how do we take them out?" Jackson asked.

Rebecca looked at Sherie. "They hate wolf shifters. We could use that to our advantage somehow."

"So, we attack?" I asked. "Draw their attention away from you?"

Sherie frowned. "I don't like the sound of that. I'd never forgive myself if something happened to one of you."

I smiled to myself, enjoying the fact these witches had developed a natural affinity and bond with us now because of their daughters.

"So, one of you focus on protecting us, while the other one takes care of the bad witches?" I suggested.

Sherie glanced at Rebecca, who nodded. "We can do that. I'm better at protection spells, anyway," she said.

Rebecca grinned. "And I'm better at attacking spells. So, bring it on!" She stretched her arms and cracked her knuckles.

"All right then, let's do this." I turned to Jackson. "Divide and conquer? I'll come at them from the north."

Jackson nodded in agreement. "I'll cover the south."

We had a plan.

The witches rolled their hands, white sparkling magic pulsing around them.

Without wasting another moment, I shifted back to my wolf form.

Jackson followed suit.

We powered toward the church.

I bounded toward the north and was confronted by a male warlock.

He stood on the steps of the church, ready and waiting. His eyes looked crazy and unnatural, swirling with silver beneath the storm that played above him.

I put my head back and howled, drawing his attention.

Without a second's hesitation he fired magic directly at me.

Thanks to my fast reflexes I dodged out of the way unscathed. Not breaking my stride, I kept running, circling closer, growling and howling, the swirling white magic of protection around me like a shield. Jumping up I saw Sherie protecting Jackson. So, I dodged around a car, only to cop a purple ball of magic in the face. Pain burned my eyes and I dropped to the ground rolling onto my back and batting at my face futilely with my paws.

Then, Sherie was beside me like an angel, casting a spell over me.

The pain eased and my eyesight came back instantly. *Fuck. That was close.* I scrambled back to my feet and charged to the front door of the church for a second time.

The warlock was there, firing balls of blinding light at Jackson. I heard him yelp, and a thud as he hit the ground.

Oh no. My stomach lurched. I leaped over the steps, running straight for the warlock—intent on ending his days—when he suddenly disappeared. I skidded to a halt and peered around. He was gone, literally nowhere to be seen.

Sherie ran across the front of the church to help Jackson where he lay on his side, blood covering his pelt.

I couldn't help him now; he was in good hands. What I needed to do was stop whoever was casting this spell. Fear aside, I burst through the front door... but no one was inside. *Strange.* Racing through the rooms and hallways, water falling from my coat onto the hardwood floors, I made my way to the inner sanctum.

Tall candles were lit and surrounded the room, casting flickering shadows everywhere. Darkness consumed each corner, and flashes of light lit up the center of the room.

Rebecca stood at one end of the space, flames of magic dancing over her hands as she fought a blonde witch I'd never seen before, as well as the warlock who, moments ago, had been standing outside attacking us.

The warlock spun around, catching her off-guard.

Rebecca was hit in the side and fell to her knees.

I heard her pained gasp and saw red. With a growl, I charged forward with all my might. Before anyone could react, I jumped, teeth bared at the two people responsible for this spell that was hurting Bella, and all those she loved.

The blonde witch lifted her hand to throw a spell at me.

The warlock grabbed her arm. Then, they were gone.

I landed on the floor where they'd been standing, throwing my head left and right, but there was no sign of them. Only dust and black magic remained where they'd once been. *Damn it.* I rushed over to Rebecca.

She knelt, gasping for air and holding her belly.

I shifted back to human, needing my voice. But Sherie wouldn't hear me in here, though. So, I raced to the nearest window, pushed it open and screamed, "Sherie! Rebecca needs help!"

Sherie came bursting through the front doors of the church.

Jackson hobbled after her, holding his arm in a strange sort of way.

She went straight for Rebecca, summoning up her magic. She ran her hands over Rebecca, and magic arched from her fingers to the other woman, sparking and sizzling.

Rebecca let out a sigh, slumping on the spot.

I hurried over to Jackson. "You okay?"

Jackson nodded, dried blood caked over his chest and shoulder. "Yeah. That bastard got me good, but Sherie saved me. She's handy in a pinch, that's for sure."

I swallowed hard. Jackson could have died. We *all* could have. "Let's check on Rebecca," I said, turning back to the witches.

Sherie had Rebecca's arm around her, trying desperately to lift her up, but not quite managing it.

She looked at me with panic written all over her face. "I have to get her back to Kathy's house. *Now.*"

I nodded. She knew best when it came to magic. "How do we do that?"

"Can you do that transportational thing?" Jackson asked, grimacing in pain. "You know the thing you did to us?"

Rebecca inclined her head. "Yes, I can. It'll take most of my power, and you may feel a little sick, but hold on, okay?"

I nodded. "Whatever you want."

Jackson grabbed hold of my arm as I bent over and lifted Rebecca up and held her against my body.

"Let's go."

Sherie reached for us, and then we flew through time and space. We landed, smack bang, back into Kathy's flood water drenched front lawn. It was like being plopped straight into a cold swimming pool.

We went under, my breath trapped in my lungs. But I got my feet beneath me and stood, grabbing hold of Rebecca and lifting her up above the freezing cold water still running through the town.

She coughed and spluttered, ushing the hair out of her face.

"What happened?" I grated out.

Sherie groaned. "Sorry. I forgot about the protection spell Kathy's running. We need to get inside the old-fashioned way."

We waded through the water and staggered up the steps. The wind and rain were thankfully gone, but the town was still flooded.

Sherie reached out and rang the doorbell.

The door flung open a heartbeat later.

"You're alive!" Bella cried, flinging herself into my arms.

I let her grip me for one precious moment, loving the feel of her warmth against me. "Yeah, but we need to get inside, beautiful."

"Oh, yes. Sorry!" Bella dragged me inside and the others followed.

"Are Tiffany and Ruby waking up?" I asked, unnecessarily because as I stepped into the house the answer to my question was revealed.

Both girls were sitting up, eyes open, but looking pale and weak.

"You're both back." I grinned as relief overwhelmed me.

Kathy lowered her arms. "Is it safe to release the spell?" she asked.

I nodded. "I think so. They're gone. Disappeared into thin air."

"Thank God for that," Kathy said. "Oh dear, but what happened?"

She rushed for Rebecca and Sherie.

I hobbled over to the couch, collapsed onto it, and threw back my head. "Fuck me, that was intense."

Bella rushed over and sat in my lap, wrapping her arms around me and sobbing. "I'm so glad you're all right."

I held her and smiled at Jonah who was looking more than a little relieved to have me back. "Everything go okay while I was gone?" I asked.

He shrugged. "You know, just the normal stuff. Witches doing spells. Magical comas. Storms, lightning, thunder."

I laughed. "Yeah, our life isn't exactly boring anymore, is it?" I glanced over at Billy who was holding Ruby close.

"She okay?" I asked, lifting my chin toward his pregnant mate.

Billy grinned. "Yep. Thanks to you four."

I glanced out the window and held my mate close. "Now, we've just got to wait and see what Elliot discovered."

There was silence in the room as everyone mulled over our words.

The witch and warlock who'd attacked our mates had disappeared, but they weren't dead, and I had the sneaking suspicion that they'd be back.

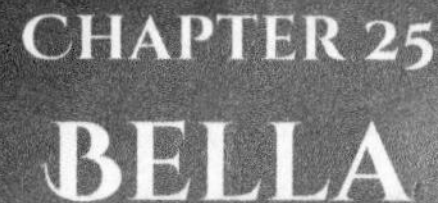

CHAPTER 25
BELLA

om and Sherie worked on Rebecca for ages, then put her into Mom's bed to rest. It was getting late, and dark, but no-one was going home. Not a chance. Our tiny house had never held so many people.

"Can we sleep here tonight?" Tommy asked. He glanced at my mom, then back at me. "That is if we're welcome?"

I nodded, then looked at Mom. "I'm exhausted. Can we set up some food for everyone, then head to bed?"

Mom nodded, then smiled. "That's a good idea, hon." She magicked up a large, long table in the middle of the room and began summoning food. The aroma of delicious hot meat pies, bowls of crispy, salted chips, steamed rice, and fragrant fried chicken soon filled the house.

I stood and stared, impressed with my mom's versatility. She didn't usually make so much at once—but then, she didn't normally need to feed a small army of witches and shifters.

When she was finally done, she said, "Dig in, everyone, please. Then we'll work out where everyone's going to sleep."

We ate as much as we were able and cleaned up.

Then Mom took over, organizing bedding for the rest of the clan.

"Good night, everyone," I called, dragging Jonah and Tommy to bed. Ironically, my room was big, but my bed was small. "Hang on a minute," I said, conjuring a small amount of magic to my fingers. Working a spell to make the bed larger, it grew until it was the size of a king, and easily took up half the bedroom now.

"Okay. I'm in the middle." I started to strip off, not caring about anything other than climbing into my bed and going to sleep. I got down to my tank and undies, stripped off my bra, then pulled back the covers.

Tommy and Jonah stared at me.

"Come on," I said, rolling my eyes. "I want both of you with me." I crawled over the bed, arranged the three pillows, and lay down with my head on the middle one.

Jonah and Tommy began to strip, though Tommy wore only the pants Mom had magicked on him when he'd arrived back here from their venture to the church.

I stared at them as their bodies were revealed to me. "You're both so beautiful."

They both blushed, simultaneously.

I giggled. *Who knew they'd be so coy?* "Come, please." I held my hands out to them, tired to the bone. I'd never felt so utterly exhausted before. I knew that if I closed my eyes for even a moment, I'd slide into a deep and blissful sleep instantly.

Jonah slid to my right and lay down.

Tommy lay down on my left.

I rolled onto my left side and laid a protective hand over Jonah. "Can you cuddle me from behind, Tommy? I have to lie on this side, sorry. Or I can't sleep."

"No problem," he said, spooning me from behind. He growled softly, his face buried in my neck.

I was too tired to react in any overt way, but feeling his hot body curl around mine was like sheer heaven. I could feel his masculinity pressing into me and sighed as I wiggled against them, glad I still had my knickers on.

He groaned and kissed my neck. "Keep doing that and you won't be wearing underwear for very long."

I sighed, smiled, and stopped wriggling. Now wasn't the time for that. "Thank you both for everything you did today." I adjusted my arm and placed my hand on Jonah's chest, my palm right over his heart.

He turned his head to look at me and smiled. "Tommy did most of it, Bella. I just stayed here."

"Exactly where I wanted you," I said, then yawned loudly. "I didn't realize how important having two mates would be until today. It was so good knowing that one of you could stay with me, while the other one went off to chase the bad guy. I would have been sick with worry if you'd left me all alone." I closed my eyes and felt sleep tugging at me through the darkness of my lashes.

"Elliot is your mate too. And he'll be back soon," Tommy whispered.

I sighed, not wanting to talk about that particular issue at the moment. Elliot was a complicated topic for me. I wanted him, but if he was the price that had to be paid to keep Jonah and Tommy by my side, then I would pay it. Even if it killed me. "Good night." I allowed sleep to claim me and dreamed of a wolf shifter running endlessly through the night, drinking from watering holes, and leaping large fences in single bounds.

THE NEXT MORNING I woke up with the covers pushed off the bed, and instead I was simply covered and wrapped in the hot arms of my mates. I blinked, trying not to move so I didn't wake them up. I couldn't believe that today was Sunday. *Has it really only been a few days since Thanksgiving?* The day before, I'd just met these men and realized they were meant to be in my life.

I had to go back to college tomorrow and the thought of normal life after what we'd gone through over the last few days just seemed wrong. And weird.

I was still lying on my left side with Tommy pressed up against my back, his arm slung possessively over my waist.

Jonah had rolled away and was flat on his belly, snoring peacefully away.

"Good morning," Tommy whispered into my ear.

I smiled as a shiver rippled through me, amazed that this all felt so normal. And *so* good. "Good morning," I said.

Tommy stroked my hips, then came up to cup my breasts beneath my tank.

Desire stirred in my belly, but I simply couldn't do more than sigh and lean into his touch. I still felt drained despite the solid sleep.

He must have felt my lack of desire because he pushed me over, so I lay on my back, and stared down at me with a worried look on his face. "Are you okay?"

I grimaced. "Yeah, I think so. But I'm so tired. I'm sorry."

He shook his head. "Never be sorry for wanting to wait, Bella. The time will be right when it's right. And I'll wait for you, forever." He leaned down and kissed me.

Jonah groaned loudly, rolling onto his back and stretching his arms above his head. "What are you guys talking about?"

I smiled at him. "Just saying how exhausted I am. And that I'm sorry all we did was sleep last night. I just... passed out."

Jonah smiled at me, then leaned over and kissed me too. "You're our mate, Bella. Your health is the most important thing to us. Everything else will happen in its own good time."

"Thanks." Despite their reassurance, I knew that I would always worry about whether I was enough for them. Perhaps that was just something I was going to have to work on personally; feeling more confident and comfortable within myself. My stomach suddenly grumbled, reminding me I hadn't eaten nearly enough last night in my exhausted state.

"Breakfast time?" Jonah said, sliding off the bed and grabbing for the clothes he'd left on the floor last night.

"Yeah," I said, not wanting to move.

Tommy bit my shoulder playfully. "Let's go, unless you want to see if we can make you come again?"

That got me moving. Not that I didn't want to experience that sort of pleasure with them again. I did, but with my body being utterly exhausted, and the worry about Elliot hanging over my head, I realized that this morning was probably not the time to try that again.

"Maybe tonight?" I asked as I pulled on some clean clothes and was rewarded with a grin. I had no idea what today held, but I was hoping I could start my life with my men soon. Guilt free. Worry free. Threat free. If that was at all possible.

We trundled down the stairs, the smell of fresh coffee in the air.

The hairs on the back of my neck stood on end. "What the..."

"What's wrong?" Tommy asked, coming up to grab my hand.

I turned around, looking for the source of the strange feeling.

"You guys ready for some breakfast?" my mom called from the kitchen, the smell of baked bread wafting toward us.

"Oh, hell yeah," Jonah said, heading off in search of food.

I looked around, uneasy. "Yeah, Mom. I just..." I had to find out where that feeling was coming from. Because I was pretty sure... *Oh, my God!* I rushed to the front door and flung it open wide.

There on the front lawn was a pile of wolves, all sleeping on the wet grass.

On the porch, was a naked, sleeping Elliot.

"Oh, my God," I breathed.

Elliot stirred, his huge body moving slowly as he woke, rolled over, and stretched out his back.

I couldn't stop staring. His body was absolutely exquisite. He was huge in every way, and his muscles looked so big and strong and thick. Then there was his dick, which I was embarrassed to admit was the largest of the three of my mates. And the most beautiful by far. It was long and thick, with a perfectly arrow-shaped head that made my insides pulse and pound with unexpected yearning. I looked away. *Damn it. Why is it that the one mate I've convinced myself I don't need, is the one whose body I want so bad?*

"Hey." Elliot pulled himself up to his feet.

I flicked my hand and conjured some black joggers on him, covering his delicious lower half. "Hey," I managed to return, trying to lift my gaze to his face, but not succeeding. *Damn, that chest...* I flicked my hand again, conjuring an ugly shapeless white t-shirt that somehow still managed to cling to his muscles in a way that made me want to run my hands all over him.

"Hey, man." Tommy went forward and embraced his friend. "How'd you go?"

Elliot hugged Tommy back for a mere second, then let him go, stepping back to point toward the front lawn. "I found them."

I fell back against the door frame and steadied myself by clinging to the wood. He'd found them. He'd found my father. *How were we ever going to repay him?*

"And you got them to come back," Tommy said. "How?"

Elliot shrugged. "Had to Dom them a bit."

"Dom them?" I repeated, staring at the three wolves still sleeping on the grass out the front of my mom's house. *Which one was my dad? The smallest one? Would he be the half warlock wolf?*

I saw some neighbors walk out their front door to grab a newspaper, then dart inside. Terrified.

Shit. We were going to have to get them inside soon or the neighbors were going to call animal rescue.

Elliot looked at me and answered my question. "I'm an Alpha, and so is Matthew. So, I had to, um, dominate him to force him to follow me."

I stared at him. "As in, you hurt him?" *He wouldn't have done that, would he?* That didn't fit with how I saw Elliot. Even with all his gruff strength, there was a good heart beneath it all, beating hard.

Elliot shook his head. "God, no. But wolves are pack animals and they respond to the strongest animal around. I just had to growl and threaten them a bit. They're all fine." He tilted his head. "Well, no. I mean they're weak, tired, And starving. But that wasn't me. That's twenty years of living in a body that's not your primary."

I didn't think I'd ever heard Elliot say so many words in a row, and I found myself captivated by his mouth. *Concentrate! Remember. You broke up with him. For his own good. For my own good. Stop looking at his lips! ...But then I promised Tommy I'd give Elliot another chance...*

I coughed to clear my throat, my mouth salivating at the smell of sweat and heat emanating off Elliot. *Focus.* "Do you think you could get them to come around the back? The neighbors are going to lose their minds if they see three wild animals hanging out in our front yard."

"Oh, yeah. Sure," Elliot said, and trotted down the steps.

I went around to the side of the house and opened the gate.

Elliot gently spoke to the wolves.

All three of them stood up and followed him around the side and past me.

One of the wolves stopped and sniffed me, staring at me like he knew me.

I stared back, my stomach aflutter.

"Um, hi," I said, my pulse pumping in my throat. Was this my... "Can he understand me?"

Elliot turned around and nodded, his face solemn. "Yeah, he can. And Bella? That's your dad, Matthew."

My mouth dropped open and I stared at the gray wolf that was almost as big as I was standing as a human.

"Oh. Well. Hi." *So eloquent.* "I'm Bella."

The wolf inclined his head as though bowing, then loped away.

I stared after him, noting the skinniness in his frame, the boniness of his back. The scars on his hide and tail made me flinch. How much trauma had he seen in his life? I locked the side gate and walked around the back to a flurry of activity. Someone must have seen us, or something, because everyone from inside the house had congregated in the back yard.

The noise was immense and the wolves seemed terrified, pressing against the back fence.

I ran forward, standing in front of them and putting my hands up. "They haven't been with people for like, twenty years. You need to back off."

Where I got the strength to stand in front of my best friends, all the moms, and the mates and yell at them, I had no idea.

Elliot came to stand beside me. "Bella's right. They need to rest, and eat. It's probably best if they come back to the pack and stay at our place, and you can all come visit in a few days."

There was an uproar from the witches, and I sighed.

"You take care of it," I said to Elliot, and left him to it. I turned around and walked over to the three cowering wolves and sat down on the ground with them.

They stared at me, then inched closer.

The arguing and sounds behind me grew quieter as I reached out and stroked the fur of my father's back. "I'm so sorry this happened to you."

He lay down and put his head in my lap. I stroked my hand through his fur, tears gathering and flowing down my cheeks unchecked.

Elliot knelt beside me. "Everyone's agreed to let them come back home with us and stay at Jackson's place because he has a better house and a bigger block."

I nodded. "That's great. Thank you." I wiped the tears from my face and turned to look up at my third mate—the one I'd rejected.

Elliot was frowning at me.

"Can we talk?" he asked quietly.

I coaxed my father's head off my lap and pushed myself to my feet. "Yes, I think we should."

Jackson shifted into his big black wolf to lead the gray wolves—our fathers—home, while the moms sobbed in pure relief and profound happiness.

Ruby went home with her men.

Tiffany stayed with my mom and hers.

I went home with Tommy, Jonah, and Elliot. It was high time we sorted out this mating triad thing, once and for all.

CHAPTER 26

BELLA

My stomach ached the whole drive back to the pack, knowing what I was going to have to say to Elliot.

I didn't need him. I couldn't possibly.

Someone like me didn't even need two men, but I would take the gift if Jonah and Tommy wanted me as well. They could share. They worked together well. They'd proven to me how much they cared about me with everything they did yesterday.

Elliot was jealous. And dominant. He could command an Alpha. That was just too much for me.

We arrived back to the small home Elliot and Tommy lived in and

I drifted inside, glancing around and wondering how this was going to work now.

Would we stay here and Elliot move out?

The idea filled me with a sadness I couldn't contain. A sob broke through and I covered my mouth to swallow hard.

No. Hold it together. This is for the best.

"Please let me go first," Elliot said, indicating the couch. "I know that you've made a decision about us, and I want you to hear me out before you try and break it off with me. Again."

I swallowed hard and nodded, hurrying over to the couch and sitting down.

Tommy and Jonah sat on the chairs around the dining room, quiet, but present. I could feel their love for me. Their support.

But they were giving Elliot time to talk, so I would allow it, too.

"You've decided to reject our mating, haven't you?" Elliot asked gently. "You've said as much, I know. But I need to be sure I understand what you meant."

I looked up, straining my neck to see him. "You're too tall up there."

Elliot sat down on the couch on the opposite side of the room.

He stared at me and waited.

I didn't want to say it all again, so I stared down at my hands clasped in my lap. "I don't think we're suited. I haven't from the start."

"Why would you think that?" Elliot asked.

I sighed and lifted my gaze to his. "Because I'm me. Haven't you noticed? I'm not strong, or confident, or like Ruby and Tiffany. I don't know what to do with three men. I'm not even sure I know what to do with one."

Elliot frowned. "I disagree."

"About which bit?" I'd made quite a few statements there.

"All of it. You are strong. You're brave, even. And I'm glad you're not like Ruby or Tiffany, because they're not meant to be my mate. You are. Which makes you perfect."

I pressed my lips together, thinking hard about what to say next. "Elliot, you're obviously not designed to live in a family like this one. Which I can completely understand. Why would you want to share your mate with other men? I'm sure that there's another woman out there designed for you. Someone who doesn't make you share your life. Someone who can handle how sexy, and big you are. But it's not me."

I looked straight at him. I was doing a good job of being strong, being selfless.

"Is that what you want?" Elliot asked, pushing off the couch and onto his knees, then crawling over to me.

I took a deep breath, ignoring the tears that swelled in my eyes, then rolled down my cheeks. I forced my voice to stay even.

"What I want..." My voice broke, and I coughed to clear it. Then tried again. "I want...to do this right. To make the hard decisions now. The love spell I cast demands a payment for its use, and I know that losing you is what I must pay.... I..."

I shook myself and sniffed loudly, casting a quick spell across my face to dry my tears and runny nose. "You'll be happier without me, Elliot. Without Jonah and Tommy in your bed. I know you will."

"How could I be happy without my mate?" he asked quietly, looking straight at me and making everything in me cry and ache. "And I won't allow you to pay that sort of spell... fee. Losing you is something I can't live with."

It wasn't fair.

I forced myself to be strong. "You don't mean that, okay? Maybe Fate got it wrong?"

Elliot got up from the floor, sat down on the couch beside me, then grabbed me and pulled me into his lap.

"What are you doing?" I asked.

"Proving to you that we're meant to be together. As a wolf, there are several things that tell us who our mate is. Number one is the scent." He bent his head forward and inhaled deeply.

He groaned, a deep, sexy sound that made my belly clench with longing.

Then he lifted his head and stared at me with those dark blue eyes.

"Then there's the instant attraction, of course." He swallowed hard, his throat working. "When I saw you for the first time in Milly's, I thought I was going to shift right then and there. Lose control like some randy thirteen-year-old boy. I'm thirty-five, Bella. I've had my share of women. But no-one, and I mean no-one, has ever made me feel the way you do."

I didn't want to ask, but I desperately needed to know. "And how's that? How do I make you feel?"

My hands moved of their own accord, sliding over his chest and pressing against his heart that beat like a steam train.

He looked deep into my eyes and said, "Like my life will end if I can't be near you."

My mouth dropped open. "But you..."

"I know. I reacted badly when I saw you with Tommy and Jonah. I was jealous as sin. I wasn't mad at you. I was mad at them. At myself. At Fate. For giving me such an incredible mate, and me not being strong enough to deal with it. You're far more than I deserve, Bella, but if you'll let me love you... If you'll give me a second chance... I'll spend my whole life proving to you that we're meant to be together."

Tears filled my eyes and spilled over.

How was I going to fight against that?

I opened my mouth and flapped my lips like a fish, the words not coming out. "But the payment... the spell?"

"Fuck the spell," he said, gripping me tight. "Let it take payment in another way. We're meant to be together. It put us together. It can't possibly tear us apart."

When I didn't respond, Elliot's face fell and he said, "Unless you don't want me? And that's why you've avoided being with me?"

"Oh, God no," I said, pressing my hands closer. "I want you."

Too much. So much. It's scary.

"You do?" he asked. "Like I want you? Because when I kissed you that one time, you freaked out and didn't want me touching you. I figured you don't find me as attractive as you do Tommy and Jonah. I know I'm big, and you're small, but I won't hurt you, I promise."

The sweet words coming out of my huge Alpha made the tears flow even faster.

I desperately wiped at them, trying to get a handle on my emotions. On my body.

This was the punishment for the love spell. Feeling things I never thought I would. Loving someone I never thought I would.

Needing to love them, aching for them. It wasn't normal. And it scared me.

"You *are* afraid of me. I knew it. It's okay... I'll just..." Elliot slid me off his lap and made to stand up.

Panic flared so hard and fast I yelled, "No!"

I pushed him back against the couch cushion and threw my leg over his waist, straddling him so I could talk to him. So he couldn't leave.

"No?" Elliot repeated, his hands sliding over my thighs and around my hips.

I shivered, feeling need and lust coil deep inside me. "I want you... in a way I can't describe. It's scary how much I need you."

Elliot groaned as though someone had torn into his heart. The time for words had come and gone. Nothing was going to reassure either of us how right we were together, until we actually felt how good and right it was.

In the biblical sense.

I swooped down, gripping Elliot's face and kissing his lips in the most awkward, artless way possible. But I hoped I got points for enthusiasm.

He moaned and grabbed my ass tight, thrusting his tongue between my lips and making me gasp.

He grabbed hold of my hips, shifted to the edge of the couch, then stood up.

I squealed, but didn't fight him, wrapping my legs around his waist and holding onto him like a limpet to a rock.

"Hold on, beautiful."

He walked us into Tommy's bedroom, then let me slide down his body, to the floor.

The door closed behind us and I looked over to see Jonah and Tommy standing by the wall.

"I assume we're all invited?" Tommy asked.

I nodded, a squeal building in my throat. "Yes. Please. I want all my mates. Together. Please."

A week ago, the idea of making love to three men at all, let alone at once, had terrified me enough to make me avoid men altogether.

Now, staring at my three soul mates, all I felt was love—and excitement.

"How do we do this?" I asked, not even sure how we got naked, let alone how I was going to take them all into me.

Elliot chuckled. "Well, it would be great if you could get rid of all our clothes at once. You up for that, my gorgeous witch?"

He said the word with such affection, I found it impossible to deny him.

I nodded, and squealed as I whipped my hand around the room, magically removing the clothing from all four of us and sending it all into a large pile in the adjoining bathroom.

I gasped and covered my breasts with my hands, the stark reality of what I'd just done coming home to roost, with tingling tight nipples, and embarrassment flooding my face.

I stared at the men, their beautiful bodies now naked. Their cocks were hard and extended in front of them in anticipation of what was about to come.

"Oh, my God," I whispered.

Elliot laughed and rushed forward, scooping me up into his arms and walking toward the bed. "Time to make you ours, Bella."

I pressed my hands to his bare chest and relaxed into my Alpha. "And for me to make you mine."

Elliot put me down onto the bed and I shuffled up, laying on my back as he prowled over the top of me. As he stared down into my eyes I saw his wolf. In the color of his eyes. In the sparkle of his teeth in his grin.

Now was not the time to be afraid.

Now was the time to embrace the wolf in me, and mate forever with the three men Fate had sent my way.

I reached up for Elliot's neck and dragged him down into a kiss.

I closed my eyes, overwhelmed by the feel of Elliot on top of me. He was pressed against me and I could feel... everything.

His cock against my thigh, pressing into me. His hard body against my soft one.

God, it felt good.

Overwhelmingly so.

I'm not sure I'm ever going to be the same after this.

Instead of being scared, I threw myself into the eye of the storm. I shifted my hips so that Elliot would lie between my thighs, and pressed my bare pussy against him.

He groaned and rolled to the side. "Damn, woman. For a virgin, you're a damn siren."

I stared at him. "Is that bad?"

He barked out a laugh. "God, no. What's bad is I'm going to struggle to control myself when you're this hot."

I didn't know what to say, so I tugged at his arm. "Come back."

"Not yet." He lifted his hand and called to the others. "Join us."

Jonah and Tommy came over and Tommy knelt at the bottom of the bed, grabbing my hips to pull me toward him.

"You're all good if I...?" Tommy asked Elliot.

I glanced at my Alpha, who grinned. "Oh, yeah. Get her as wet as possible."

Tommy dove between my thighs and I screamed as his mouth covered my pussy. "Oh, God!"

Elliot turned my head toward him and captured my lips with his.

I groaned and opened to him, letting his tongue sweep into my mouth as Tommy did magical things to my clit.

Jonah's hands were on my breasts, tweaking my nipples and rolling the sensitive flesh with his fingers.

The pleasure went on and on as they loved me from every angle.

I gasped after what felt like hours, breaking off from Elliot's kiss. It was too much. I was aching, deep inside.

"Can you put your fingers inside? Please?" I asked Tommy, wanting some relief from the pressure.

Tommy pulled away and Elliot said, "Oh, no. That's not the way you're coming this time."

He rolled on top of me and spread my thighs wide.

I lifted my legs, wanting to feel him where I was aching.

I stared up at him.

He held his weight on his arms. "You ready?"

I nodded. "Yes. Please."

I pulled at his arms and he grabbed his cock and positioned it at my entrance.

I gasped, my whole world zeroing in on that one spot between my thighs. I felt the thick head nudge my lips and I opened my thighs wider, wanting him inside me.

I knew it would hurt, but damn, the waiting was hurting more.

"Please, hurry!" I arched my back, urging him closer.

He surged forward in one long thrust.

I cried out, turning my head away to groan as he filled me completely. There was pain, but there was much more. A rightness. A deep pleasure. A bliss that no-one ever told me would exist when my mate finally made me his.

Oh, my God.

Tears tingled the edges of my eyes.

"Did I hurt you?" Elliot whispered from above.

I wanted to answer him, but I couldn't speak. I tossed my head from side to side to say no. I couldn't say the words. My throat was too tight with emotion.

I dug my nails into his arms, then reached down to grab his ass, finally opening my eyes to see him hovering above me, worried.

I swallowed hard. "Please. More."

The worry disappeared and he pulled away, only to drive home harder, and faster. I cried out, this time from pure pleasure.

Oh, God. I was going to cum so quickly. I could already feel the tightening in my belly.

Elliot's massive body rolled over mine and I lifted my legs to wrap them around his waist as he rode me faster and faster.

It was such an amazing feeling to be filled by him, to ache so much for that deep penetration and feel his body inside mine.

"Oh.. I..." I started to peak, so I grabbed onto his huge arms and threw my head back, gripping him as he thrust deep one more time.

My orgasm released, pulsing pleasure through me.

I screamed as Elliot groaned above me, biting into the side of my neck as he spilled himself inside me.

Hot pulses of his seed filled me and I cried out with the beauty of it all.

I pulled him down, wanting to feel the weight of him on top of me. He panted with exertion.

He rolled us onto the side and kissed me, before withdrawing and slowly moving away, a smile on his face.

"Wow," I said, wiping the sweat from my brow.

Then I looked to the side, where Tommy was waiting.

"You up for taking me, too?" he asked.

I nodded and held out my arms.

He grinned. "Jump on top."

He reached over and took me by the waist, flipping me over and pulling me up so I straddled him, then I looked down on his smiling face.

"How do I do this?" I said, glancing back at his thighs behind me, and wriggling over the thick cock that lay beneath me.

He chuckled. "Slide back a bit."

I did and he grabbed his cock in his hand and held it vertical. "Now go up and slide down on it."

I frowned, but pushed back, tilting my pelvis and feeling for the edge of him. As I moved back, he thrust up.

"Oh." When I felt him inside me, I slid down, his cock filling me up and my newly sensitized tissues relaxing around him. "Wow."

This was different.

Tommy grinned and cupped my breasts, stroking his thumbs over my nipples, then taking hold of my hips and moving me up and down.

"Ride me, beautiful."

I smiled down at him, enjoying taking some of the control as I moved up and down, but the more I moved, the tighter his grip on me became.

I gasped, not sure this was working for me. "I think I need more."

He grinned. "Hold on."

He flipped me over and once again I was on my back, Tommy driving into me.

Now this was what I wanted. I lifted my legs, taking him deeper and grabbing onto his shoulders, pulling him closer. Our lips met and I stroked my tongue along the seam, thrusting into his mouth and loving it when he sucked on my tongue.

The tingles were beginning to grow again, then Tommy's motions began to change, becoming jerky.

I pulled him into me, grabbing onto his tight ass, moaning as he filled me with his seed, mixing with Elliot's and making me ache for so much more.

Tommy kissed my lips and rolled onto his side, taking his weight off me.

I panted, exhausted in the best possible way. But the tingles in my belly called to me for more. Just one more.

Tommy kissed my nipple as he lay beside me, stroking his hand possessively over my hip.

I sat up on the bed. Jonah stood nearby, looking sheepish. Well, as sheepish as one can with an erection in hand.

"I'm assuming you want to wait until you're healed to take me?" Jonah asked. "I don't want to hurt you."

I glanced at Jonah's cock. He was smaller than Tommy and Elliot, which was a relief more than anything. *Perfect.*

"I want you, too," I said.

He walked forward, bent over, and kissed me gently.

"How about you roll over and get on all fours?" he whispered against my lips.

"Um, all right," I said, though the idea of sticking my butt in the air seemed a bit weird to me.

I turned over onto my hands and knees.

Jonah put his hands on me, stroking over my back and my ass.

"Open your legs for me, beautiful." He stroked the insides of my thighs until I opened for him.

"Good girl. Perfect."

He pushed on the small of my back, so I dropped down, then felt the tip of his cock at the entrance to my body.

That's what he wants.

I dropped my face closer to the blankets on the bed and pushed back.

He slid into me gently and I gasped out my pleasure at feeling the pressure of his cock from this angle.

Definitely different.

And awesome.

I sighed as he began moving in and out of me, stroking the fire Tommy had begun.

I grabbed for the bedding, my hands filling with nothing but blankets.

"Tommy. Elliot. Can you both come here?" I gasped. "Hold my hands. Please."

They climbed onto the bed, each of them lying down beside me.

Tommy gripped my left hand and Elliot gripped my right.

Elliot kissed the back of my neck, while Tommy reached under and cupped my breast with his hand.

"Oh, God!" I cried out, pleasure washing over me as my second orgasm crashed into me. I quivered and squeezed Jonah's cock.

Jonah groaned and began to move faster, harder. Fucking me the way I needed him to.

"More," I cried out. "More! Please."

There was one final orgasm moments away. I was sliding down a slippery slope. My skin was dotted with sweat. My pussy ached as he fucked me over and over.

Elliot slipped his hand beneath my belly, finding my clit and flicking the aching bud over and over again.

I began to scream into the mattress as the pleasure built and built, higher and higher.

"I'm gonna blow." Jonah gasped. "I can't hold on anymore."

I didn't want him to, but I couldn't say the words.

Jonah thrust his cock into me one more time, pushing me to the very precipice of the orgasmic cliff. There I hung. Time stood still.

Then Jonah began to cum, his orgasm pushing me through my

own and I convulsed over and over again, safe in the arms of the three men I loved.

When Jonah finally pulled away, I was cocooned and dragged up to the pillows. I closed my eyes and grabbed for my men, wanting to feel all of them.

Tommy pressed a kiss to my forehead and I opened my eyes. "I love you," I managed to say, then twisted around. "I love all of you."

Elliot tugged my face to his for another kiss and I let my thoughts float away. I would never regret choosing my three mates.

The men Fate, and my Halloween magic, had sent to me.

You can pre-order book 3:
https://books2read.com/wolf-magic

Or read on for a sneak peek...

WOLF MAGIC

TIFFANY

Within moments of hanging up the phone, Mom used a transportation spell to get to me. After seeing the state of Ruby and deducing it came from a magical source, we didn't call the hospital. Instead, she called all the moms, and Bella. Within an hour, we had both generations together.

"Do you know what's wrong with her?" I asked Sherie, Ruby's mom, who was waving her hands over her daughter, analyzing the problem, white sparkling magic coursing over Ruby's body.

My mom stepped up next to me and squeezed my hand. "We

don't know, honey. Sherie's doing a spell to stabilize Ruby, but from what we can tell the pregnancy is, um, draining the life out of her."

I spun around and stared at her, aghast. "Are you telling me the baby's killing her?"

That couldn't be true. Surely all pregnant moms felt like their life was being drained by their baby? Wasn't the first trimester always the worst?

Sherie dropped her hands and sighed, turning toward me with tears in her eyes. "Ruby's carrying a daughter, but the curse on the pack means that no daughters are allowed to be born from this generation. Ruby's strong. She's managed so far, but I'm not sure how much longer the baby—or her—will last."

Sherie bit her lip and stared at my mom, tears glistening in her scared eyes. "Do you think I should... if it would save her..."

I glanced between the two moms, trying to work out what they were referring to.

When neither one spoke, only continued to stare at each other in long, knowing looks, I threw my hands up and said, "What are you talking about?"

Bella walked forward, a tear stain on one cheek. "They might be able to save Ruby, if they terminate the pregnancy."

"No!" I raced over to stand by Ruby who lay in the bed, helpless. She couldn't speak for herself, so I'd have to do it for her.

Not that I would physically be able to stop the moms if they really wanted to do it. They were much stronger than me. I was only half-witch, and had never really cared that much about perfecting my craft. I was a half-assed witch at the best of times.

But I could see how much pain was on both their faces, and used that knowledge to my advantage.

"You can't do it. You can't kill Ruby's baby!" I repeated. "She will never forgive you if you do."

The front door opened, and men's voices rang out through the house. "Ruby! You home, honey?"

"How are you feeling?" called another male voice. "Any better?"

Bella stared at the bedroom door, a look of worry on her face.

I clung to Ruby's headboard and called out, "We're in here!"

Two of Ruby's men stepped into the room, passing through one at a time. Jackson had to turn his shoulders slightly to the side as he passed through since he was so big. Darren didn't have a hope of sliding past him.

"What's going on?" Jackson asked, lingering near the doorway.

Darren hurried straight over to the bed, comfortable enough to come into the room with a full coven of witches hovering around his mate. But Darren was part-warlock, so he was always more comfortable around us than the other full-blooded wolves.

"Is she okay?" Darren asked, reaching out for one of Ruby's hands and touching her fingers. "Shit, she's deathly cold."

Bella's mom, Kathy, stepped up and said, "We're pretty sure the pregnancy's killing her. So, we need to decide if we roll the dice and wait and see what's going to happen... or..."

She let the word hang in the air, until Jackson took a step in the room and said, "Or, what?" His voice was rough with emotion. "We can't lose Ruby. I don't care what you have to do."

"We need to abort the pregnancy," Kathy said.

Darren gasped, and Jackson's face flashed with sharp pain, before he clenched his jaw and nodded once. "Do it."

I gasped at him.

"Jackson, you don't mean that!" I turned to Darren, who'd climbed onto the bed and was lying down next to his mate, brushing her long red hair away from her face. "Darren!"

He stared at me, his eyes shimmering with unshed tears. "We can't lose Ruby, Tiff. We can't. The three of us would die."

I wasn't sure if he meant it literally, but from the heavy feeling in the room, and the hardness in Jackson's face, they might.

I stomped my foot, unwilling to give up. "No! Ruby will kill us if we do it! And that's assuming she survives the process." I glared at the moms. "Can you guarantee that you can save her if you kill her baby?"

Mom glanced at Sherie. "We... can't. We don't know how tightly entwined Ruby and her daughter are with the spell. If we sever the connection, we could kill them both."

Jackson groaned and turned away, grabbing a hold of the door frame and squeezing so hard the wood cracked beneath his fingers.

I turned to Bella. Surely, she'd be on my side. "Come on, Bell! There has to be another way."

Bella chewed her lip before replying. "Well, I suppose we could do some sort of temporary stasis spell. We might be able to hold her like this for a few days. Maybe more. But any longer, and you'll endanger the fetus anyway. It needs time to grow and change, and keeping them like that too long will kill the baby."

"Why would you do that?" Darren asked from the bed.

"It would give us time to figure out what's going on," Bella said. "Maybe even find a way to break the curse once and for all."

"But you've been working on it for a month, and haven't gotten anywhere yet," Darren said, his tone speaking of despair.

I wanted to shake him, shake them all. There was no way Ruby would give up this easily. If she wasn't in a coma right now, she'd slap them all silly.

I glared at him. "It's the best hope we have, unless you can think of anything else that might save her?"

I glanced from Darren, to my mom, to Sherie, to Jackson.

They all shook their head, or stared at the floor, unable or unwilling to look at me.

I took a deep breath, knowing that I was right in my determination to try and save them both. I knew that the fetus was young, and technically Ruby and her mates could try again for another baby, if they saved Ruby.

But she would never forgive us, or her mates, for killing her daughter. I knew my friend, and that was a certainty.

I closed my eyes and inside my mind I saw Ruby, cradling her infant daughter in her arms. She was a beautiful cherub with blonde hair and blue eyes, and my friend loved her more than anything in the world.

I wasn't taking that away from her.

I opened my eyes, tears spilling down my face as my heart ached with pain, realizing how far away from that vision we were.

I brushed away the tears. "We're saving them both. I don't care what we have to do. This curse was built from a place of ignorance and hatred. Surely the love you two have for your mates, and our moms have for our dads, is enough to break it."

"It hasn't been enough so far," Bella said, "unless the spell needs you to find your mates, too?"

She smiled gently at me, and the soft joke made me sigh. "It might, but I think I've met every wolf in town now. Twice. My mates don't live here. Or they're not from this pack."

The room went deathly quiet, then the front door opened and closed again. "Hey, Ruby!"

Billy walked into the room wearing a leather jacket and I couldn't help the admiration that flowed through me. Of all Ruby's mates, Billy was my favorite: quiet, strong, sexy. Classic bad boy.

His expression fell. "What happened?"

We filled him in, and by the time we'd finished, he was sitting on the blanket box, with his head in his hands, looking just as miserable as I felt.

"You have to save her," he said quietly, and when he looked up, his eyes flashed yellow with his wolf.

"Hey. Calm down. It's okay," Jackson said, squeezing Billy's shoulder.

Billy jumped up. "It's not okay. How are we meant to...?"

He stopped, swallowing audibly as he struggled to contain his emotions.

Bella, who in the past would have run from such a strong,

emotional male, stepped closer. I watched her in admiration. Having two alpha mates had really changed her.

"Billy. We're going to try and save both of them, but I've got a hunch that the only way we're gonna break this spell, is when all three of us have found our mates. Can you think of anyone that Tiffany hasn't met that she should? Or maybe she needs to meet some guys from other packs?"

"You really think us three finding our wolf shifter mates will break the curse?" I repeated. Was Bella serious?

I crossed my arms over my chest, not liking the way they were talking about me. Like I was a problem or something. Or my singledom was part of the curse. Though if someone would point me in the right direction of my mates, I'd be grateful.

Bella nodded. "I think it's definitely a part of it. Think about what happened when I found my mates. Tabitha and David tried to kill us! The closer we get to finding love and happiness, the closer we get to destroying that spell."

I wasn't so sure about that. Tabitha had said the spell was grounded in us, but could love really break a spell that in the past we had assumed only our deaths could?

"You know I've tried everything, Bella," I grumbled. It wasn't like I hadn't tried to find my mates.

Billy jumped to his feet. "Hang on a second! I didn't even think..."
He turned to look at Jackson.

"What are you talking about?" Jackson asked.

"I was coming back to tell you I just saw Jase, and Ollie and Fin. They're home for Christmas."

I frowned. I didn't recognize any of those names. "Who are they?"

"Do you think it's possible?" Jackson asked Billy, ignoring my question.

"Why not?" Billy said. "They're three wolf shifters. All betas."

"They're all gray, too," Darren said from the bed.

I turned toward him.

"What do you mean?" I was shaking now, and I wasn't sure why. I wasn't afraid, or cold. "What's that got to do with anything?"

"You're right!" Billy said, moving closer to the bed, excitement catching in his voice. He turned to me. "Do you remember at Thanksgiving? We were talking about the fact that all of Ruby's mates are white wolves..."

"Yeah, and all of Bella's are black." I shrugged. "And I joked that mine would be all brown..."

"Or gray!" Billy said, casting a worried look at Ruby.

I frowned. "Yeah, but you said that there weren't any gray wolves in your generation."

Or he'd said they were unusual, or something like that.

Darren sat up. "They're super-rare. There are only three gray wolves in our whole pack our age, and they're three best friends, all betas."

My heart pounded faster, a premonition-type wave flowing over me, making me shiver. "Then why haven't I met them?"

Darren glanced at Billy, who said, "Because last year they left the pack. They got frustrated at being single, and said they were going to go look for their mates, and they took off. They've been all over the country, I heard."

I bit my lip. What if they'd brought home a woman, or three?

"Do you really think they could be my mates?"

Jackson laughed. "Only one way to tell. Let's go introduce you."

I glanced at my mom, who nodded. "Go. We'll get to work on the stasis spell. See if we can hold Ruby and her baby long enough that we can break the curse that binds you all."

Bella hurried over to me. "I'll come with you. The moms can look after Ruby."

I grabbed Bella's hand. "Thanks."

I needed the support.

The guys all stopped by the bed to kiss Ruby and whisper to her. I tried not to listen out of respect for their privacy.

Once they were done, they charged out the door and Bella and I followed, hopefully to fulfil a date with destiny.

You can continue reading in book 3:
https://books2read.com/wolf-magic